The Mirror Of Dùmsaro

Book Four of *The Seven Wars*

E. H. Kindred

A Novel Of The Somadàrsath

ISBN-13: 978-0985753054 (Sun Hawk Press)
ISBN-10: 0985753056

Typeset in: Crimson
Drop Caps in: Preciosa
Display text in: Metamorphous
Phonetic Transcriptions in: Junicode

The Seven Wars Series

The Immortal
Bound By Blood
Through Death Or Through Darkness
The Mirror of Dùmsaro
The Court Of The Hydra King
Time's Shadows
Storms Westward

Contents of This Volume

The Mirror Of Dùmsaro 7
Map 295
Aetherian Script 298
Glossary and Pronunciation Guide 299

All the hapless silent lovers,
All the prisoners in the prisons, all the righteous and the wicked,
All the joyous, all the sorrowing, all the living, all the dying,
Pioneers! O pioneers!

I too with my soul and body,
We, a curious trio, picking, wandering on our way,
Through these shores amid the shadows,
with the apparitions pressing,
Pioneers! O pioneers!

Lo, the darting bowling orb!
Lo, the brother orbs around, all the clustering suns and planets,
All the dazzling days, all the mystic nights with dreams,
Pioneers! O pioneers!
...
Has the night descended?
Was the road of late so toilsome? did we stop discouraged,
nodding on our way?
Yet a passing hour I yield you in your tracks to pause oblivious,
Pioneers! O pioneers!

Til with sound of trumpet,
Far, far off the daybreak call—hark! how loud and clear
I hear it wind,
Swift! to the head of the army! —swift! spring to your places,
Pioneers! O pioneers!

—Walt Whitman
Excerpted from "Pioneers! O pioneers!"

Chapter One

The kingdom was in a state of joyous celebration. For the past week, the land had been ringing with the sound of singing and music. It was the first time in hundreds of years they were truly safe. The rebel Vortearigan, who had waged war for centuries, who had once brought the kingdom of Etheria to its knees, had been defeated. His defeat was brought about by the single greatest union to ever stand together in the history of the kingdom; an alliance of seven races, their victory solidifying their friendship and issuing in what everyone expected to be a new age of prosperity and peace.

Celebrating both the victory and the new year, the High King Lavancer hosted a week of lavish festivals and feasts, inviting all of the United races to attend and share in the joy. The castle, its courtyard, and the fields beyond teemed with laughter and dancing. While all of the races were invited inside, there were mostly humans, as the larger races, such as the dragons, simply couldn't get into the castle with so many people. Likewise, the centaurs, unicorns and moranters opted to stay out in the courtyard, preferring the open space. Most of the griffins stayed outside as well, perching on the ramparts, except for their leader, Ossifer, who muscled his way inside in search of the best wine. Some of the fairies ventured into the hall, keeping their wings tucked low so to not take up too much space.

The castle was bustling that night with feasting and laughing. The early spring air was cool, and all of the windows were open to allow the crisp breeze inside. It was the final night of the celebrations, and the Great Hall was full of people in elegant costumes of all colors.

There was one man in the hall who drew many glances over the course of the evening. It was not because of the rich red coat he wore, embroidered with fine gold stitching. Nor was it because of his skin, which was as pale as the moon rising in the east, seeming a stark contrast to the velveteen black of his hair that fell across his shoulders. Nor, for once, was it because of his eyes, eyes as red as the blood he had spilled on the battlefield. It was because this man was Lask, and it was he who had slain Vortearigan and brought the kingdom together.

Lask sat at the nobles' table, at the right hand of the

king where he always sat, but he was aware of all the eyes in the hall that fell upon him with a new interest, and he sat proud and calm under their inspection, not showing that so many glances made him uneasy. It had been that way for the past week, and he supposed he was starting to get used to being watched, and thought it was only fair, as he had always watched everyone else with keen, inspecting, eyes. As the Protector, he kept a constant vigil over the safety of the king and the kingdom.

"Smile," said his wife, Myranda, from beside him, "You look a lot less scary that way."

Lask gave her a fond smile and replied,

"I don't like people watching me eat."

"It's the last night," she answered. "We'll be back home in the peace and quiet all by ourselves tomorrow."

Lask was looking forward to the day. While he enjoyed the merriment at the castle, he missed the quiet evenings by the fire when it was just him and Myranda, and it had been a long time since he'd been able to sit in a moment of absolute peace, not having the worries of war upon his shoulders.

"Dance with me," Myranda said when the meal had ended and the music began. She tugged at his hand with an enticing smile.

Lask obliged, leading her down from the nobles' table onto the main floor among the other couples. They stepped around the hall, admiring the general splendor amid the merry tune and the rhythmic stepping of so many feet. Myranda twirled away from him as the dance changed partners and Lask found himself across from the Head Ambassador.

"Fiora," he said with a smile, drawing her to him into the step, "You're looking particularly lovely."

"And you are as eerily dashing as always," she replied with a teasing smile. "Your victory has brought you many admirers. You should count yourself lucky that you're already married, else you'd surely have your hands full."

Lask gave her a crooked, roguish smile, at which Fiora couldn't help but laugh.

"Now if only we can keep it this way," said the ambassador, "With the peace. I certainly hope no one decides to take their chance and disrupt our happiness; the Hydras or the Wraiths, for example."

"I hope they give us at least a month," Lask replied, "Though I do think we should take up negotiations with the Hydras soon, particularly given the way they responded when we invited them to join the United."

"That will be an interesting discussion, to be sure," muttered the ambassador.

She spun away from him as the partner change came again, and Lask turned to find himself standing across from his best friend, the general.

"How did that happen?" asked Forge.

"You never were very good at dancing," Lask remarked.

The two decided to walk alongside each other in the general flow of the room, so to not get in the other couples' way.

"What was that you were speaking to Fiora about?" asked Forge. "You both looked so serious all of a sudden."

"The Hydras," Lask replied.

"Honestly, you can't even enjoy the peace for a week before you start worrying about another war," Forge said, giving him an accusing nudge with his elbow.

"Can't help myself."

Forge shook his head and wandered off the dance floor for a drink. Myranda soon returned to her husband.

"Leave it to Forge to throw off one of the simplest steps," she said with a fond smile.

Lask chuckled, pulling her back to him, leading her in a turn about the room. As he led her, he looked over her shoulder, seeing a faint, green curl of smoke winding up from between the stone in the floor, almost lost between the flurry of dancing feet. Myranda noticed his expression darken and looked back, catching sight of it as well.

"What is that?" she asked.

The smoke was thickening, drawing more attention,

and people were stopping in the midst of the dance to draw back from it. Lask let go of Myranda, working his way through the crowd toward it. Myranda followed in his wake, but before they could reach it, there was a blinding flash of green light and a bellowing crack of thunder. Several people screamed in the chaos. When the light cleared, they could see that something had appeared in the middle of the floor.

It was a mirror, at least twelve feet high, with its grey-black frame stretching even taller. The frame was carved with pointed knotwork, ordinarily beautiful designs, but twisted and sharpened into something far more sinister. At the base of the mirror was carved a series of Aetherian symbols, a language few could still read. And though it was a mirror, it reflected nothing.

A face appeared in the glass; a hideous, gaunt face, with a hooked nose and skin sunken under sharp cheekbones, as if it were a skull that had been hurriedly covered in stretched greyish skin. Dark brows furrowed over black eyes that glinted with unnatural reflections as it glanced around the room. Lank, wavy dark hair fell about its head.

"Such a lovely evening," said the face, in a cold voice that carried a subtle hiss.

The hall had gone deathly silent and Lask had already positioned himself between the mirror and the king, so when the mirror's black eyes fell on him, it gave a slight, sneering smile.

"Ah yes, our dear Protector. I suppose I ought to thank you. If you and your king had not opened the door several weeks ago, I might still be imprisoned." Its dark eyes surveyed the room, taking in the wide-eyed faces. "Such shock and horror," it remarked with a certain satisfied note, "I suppose there must be many dark legends about the Mirror of Dùmsaro."

A hushed murmur of gasps and whispering went up from the crowd. Lask was still, waiting for the Mirror to make a move, as he was sure it would. He was poised, ready to spring, though he knew not what he could do.

Everyone in the room started when there was crash, but it did not come from the Mirror. The doors of the hall had been blown inward, crashing back against the walls with the wind of another figure's arrival. The crowd parted in an instant as the newcomer came galloping down the center of the room, hooves clanging against the floor, leathery wings flared, dragon-like head reared back in a roar. Before he could reach the Mirror, the green light flared again and the Mirror was gone, disappeared as quickly as it had come.

"Damn it all!" swore the creature, coming to a prancing halt. His long scorpion tail swayed back and forth behind him, agitated. Everyone in the room knew this drokamerdor; he was Chai Karan, the Ancient Time. He turned his head, leathery frill flaring as he snapped, "Get everyone out. Now!"

The room hesitated, but Lask agreed with the Ancient and called,

"Everyone outside."

As the guests roused themselves out of their stunned stupor they made a quick exit out of the hall. In the midst of the bustle, Chai Karan said,

"Réasdar, Somadar, please stay."

Lask and Lavancer hung back, bidding a temporary goodbye to their wives. When the hall was empty, the Ancient turned to them. He inspected the king first, with shrewd, penetrating eyes. Lavancer shifted under his scrutiny, uneasy, until the drokamerdor's gaze swung over to Lask. He studied him for a moment, then said,

"Good God."

Lask glanced to the side, not knowing how to respond.

"How could you?" asked Chai Karan, shaking his head in disgusted disbelief.

"We were following an old map under the castle," Lask replied, defensive under the Ancient's scorn, "We had no idea—"

"Not *you,*" Chai Karan growled, but still looked straight at him to spit, "How *dare* you?"

Lask exchanged a confused glance with Lavancer.

"Lask," said Chai Karan, "You must come with me into the Void for a moment. There is something we must do."

"Into the Void?" Lask echoed, uncertain.

"Yes, come. We won't waste any time that way. Time shall stop the moment I leave. Come, put your hand on my shoulder."

Lask was reluctant, but nonetheless stepped forward to lay a chalk white hand upon the Ancient's chestnut coat. Everything seemed to lurch and Lask felt his stomach drop, then all of a sudden, everything was gone. There was complete silence, and only flat, endless grey stretching in all directions. Lask had been here before, in the brief moments when he stepped through the Gate to pass between Etheria and Earth, but now, the nothingness endured, unbroken.

"You may remove your hand," said Chai Karan, voice deafening in the utter silence. "The denizens of the Void will not dare approach me."

Lask obeyed, stepping back a bit, feeling lost and not knowing just what kind of *denizens* might be lurking about. Chai Karan's head swung around, fixing him with that sharp emerald-eyed stare to snap,

"Get out here *right now*."

"What are you talking about?" Lask asked, startled

and confused.

"Not you," snarled Chai Karan. "He knows who I'm talking to. Get out here *now*!"

Lask shook his head, wondering if the Ancient Time was in complete possession of his senses, when all of a sudden, he was swept with a strange feeling. Lask felt suddenly hot and feverish, and a wave of nausea swept over him. His breath came quicker and he heard himself gasping, feeling as though he couldn't get enough air (he had the terrible thought that perhaps there *was* no air in Void and he just hadn't noticed before). His hands started to shake, the tremor continuing up his arms and down his back, and he was forced to his knees with the sudden dizziness and nausea. He doubled over, coughing, sputtering, feeling like he was drowning, until all of a sudden, he gasped in an enormous breath.

As he exhaled, a strange, white glowing mist passed out of his mouth, following the curls of his breath, drifting up to form into a glowing ball of light beside him.

"How *dare* you?" snarled Chai Karan at the orb.

Lask looked up at the Ancient, then to the light, not knowing what was going on. His surprise was complete when the ball of light replied,

"Oh, don't sound so indignant."

"How could you take the Uniter?" demanded Chai Karan, "Do you have any idea what you might have done?"

"Yes, I have a perfectly good idea of that," answered the light, in a distinctly masculine voice that Lask found somehow familiar. "I have saved his life—several times, I might add; poor fellow is just a beacon for trouble—and continued the Prophecy as it was meant to be. Why, without me, none of it might have happened."

"Don't you dare try to take credit for the workings of the Plan—"

"Wouldn't *dream* of trying to steal *your* glory, old boy. We all know Time's supposed to be the one who brings it all around. But what you might not know, is that I have an equally important part—"

"Hardly. You are the seventh of us, last Created—"

"Always save the best for last, I say—"

Lask had picked himself up and demanded,

"Would someone kindly tell me what is going on?"

Chai Karan's head snapped back over to look at him, snarling,

"This fool has—"

"Oh, do shut it, would you?" said the light.

"Then *you* tell him," growled Chai Karan.

"Don't mind if I do," the light answered, sounding pleased. "Now then, my dear Lask, what do you know about Ancients?"

"They are the seven basic functions of the world,"

Lask replied, "Time, Life, Death, Good—"

"Evil, Mystery, and the Gateway," finished the light. "Yes. And what else?"

"They each have physical forms within Etheria to carry out their functions, the functions that drive the course of history and allow the One's Plan to be carried out."

"Precisely. You always were so very smart, one of the many reasons I like you."

"We were each allowed to choose a body," said Chai Karan, with an irritated glance at the light, "At the Beginning when we were put into the world. I took the form of a drokamerdor, Death a dragon, Mystery a human woman, and so on. However, there was one of us who couldn't make up his mind. He couldn't decide on a form to have forever, so he chose to take hosts instead."

"Hosts?" Lask echoed.

"Yes. He would bind himself to the mind of another, often unbeknownst to them, and thus anchor his function to the world through their body. It accomplishes the same end, but he can only use his power vicariously through them, and that's only after the host has become aware of his presence. He usually makes himself known, but sometimes he finds it best to keep quiet and hidden. Though how he manages that with his incessant jabbering, I'll never know."

"I have many talents," said the light, sounding smug, "You should know that."

"Wait," Lask said, catching on. He motioned at the light. "Are you telling me that you are—?"

"The Ancient Gateway," finished the light, "Keeper of the keys, responsible for the passageways between the four worlds… among other things." Lask could hear the proud grin in the voice.

"I've been host to an Ancient?" Lask asked, stunned. "For how long?"

"About four hundred years now," answered the light.

Lask let out a disbelieving breath, which sounded like a half-scoff, half-sob. For almost half his life, he'd had another being living inside him and not even known it.

"Why?" he asked after a moment.

"An excellent question," growled Chai Karan, turning impatient eyes back to the light.

"I thought you'd need the help," the light replied. "After all, you have such a big part in the Prophecy!" A glare from Chai Karan silenced any more the Gateway might have said on the subject. "And," the light continued, "I've been helping you. You always had a good intuition, but I've been making it even keener. Not to mention I've helped you survive things, given you stamina in battle, such as with Galator. I even kept you alive after Vortearigan stabbed you. You heard my voice that day, do you remember? And then afterward you were telling Myranda how you'd like to find out who had spoken to you and thank him. You always were such a dear—"

"And you always did meddle in things," Chai Karan snarled.

"Chai Karan, old friend," said the Gateway, "Surely you know the Seven Wars Prophecy, and surely you know the Mirror of Dùmsaro was supposed to be next?"

"Yes, of course, I did."

"Then how, pray tell, would that ever happen, if only an Ancient can open the door? Contrary to popular belief, you don't always know *everything*."

Chai Karan was silent, sour at the knowledge of not having made the connection.

"You see?" said the Gateway. "I've got it all under control. When Lask and Lavancer went exploring under the castle, they found the Mirror's cell, and when Lask touched the door, I just released a bit of magic and undid a few of the bindings. The Mirror did the rest. Sorry about shocking your arm that day, Lask."

Lask's brow furrowed.

"You released it?" he said. "*Why?*"

"It has to happen," answered the Gateway. "The future depends on it. Besides, it was only imprisoned because the First didn't have the means to destroy it during their time."

"And we have those means now?" Lask said.

"Yes, of course. Now then, what say we go get started taking care of this mess? Hold still, Lask, I'll take a moment to resituate myself—"

"No," Lask said, forceful and taking a step back. "I do not want to be host to an Ancient."

"What?" The light sounded hurt and forlorn. "Why? I need a place to stay in the world. I can be an even greater help to you now that you know I'm there. We could—"

"*No,*" Lask said. "If you have indeed shared my mind all these years, then you should know I am a man who needs his space and freedom. If I cannot even have that space in my own body and mind—"

"But you still have so much left to go through! You need someone to look out for you, to help you through it all—"

"Why can't you help me in your *own* body?" asked Lask.

"A question we've been asking him since the Beginning," said Chai Karan, looking smug.

"But I like having someone else's mind to keep me company. And how could I ever just pick *one* body? There's so much I like about so many of them—"

"If you can ask for any body you want," said Lask, "Why not just combine all the elements of your hosts that you liked into one?"

"I must say, I never thought of that," the light remarked, intrigued. "Such an ingenious fellow you are."

"No," Chai Karan said, "We were to pick one of the races—"

"The Creator never said that. He just said to ask for a body of our choosing."

"Really, Gateway—"

"Might want to step back for a moment."

Chai Karan huffed and stood still, stubborn, but Lask obeyed, backing up into the nothingness, as the light began to chant,

"Bruste Aucre, é rogantiel sérm fànre cùl mém més estruriòn..."[1]

Chai Karan was shaking his head, but the orb of light repeated the phrase over and over, and the light began to pulse with the rhythm of his speech. The orb began to break its spherical shape, tendrils of light twisting and coiling out of it, whipping in all directions. Chai Karan, though still disapproving, backed up out of reach. The light grew brighter as it moved faster and faster, until it flared so brightly, Lask had to shut his eyes. When he looked again, the light was gone. In its place was a strange creature.

He stood as tall as Lask did, perhaps even taller, on

---

[1] "Powerful Creator, I beseech you to make me a body of my own."

two legs like a man, with a humanoid torso, arms and hands, though his body was covered in thick white fur with black stripes. A long fluffy tail hung down behind him, with two gold barbs on the end. A pair of golden, leathery wings sprouted from his shoulders, matching the tall ears that pricked up on the top of his head. His head was that of a white tiger, with deep blue eyes and pointy-toothed jaws revealed in a broad grin. He was naked, except for a leather bandolier that stretched across his chest, bearing four keys, two of them gold, the other two black iron. He seemed to realize he was naked, bringing his tail up to cover himself, saying,

"Oh dear." He waved a hand over himself, and he was instantly covered in a flowing white robe with a tall blue collar. Waves of various shades of blue adorned the hem and the edges of the wide sleeves. He shifted around in it, bringing the bandolier out to drape over himself so that it sat outside the robe. When he was done arranging himself, he gave a satisfied nod and announced, "Much better."

"What have you done to yourself?" Chai Karan demanded.

"I took Lask's suggestion and combined my favorite features of all my hosts. Rather dashing, don't you think?" He struck a pose that flexed his muscles and showed off his form.

"You look like a total loon," growled the drokamerdor, "But I suppose now it will have to do. You'll need a name."

"Gonamadé, I think," replied the Gateway. "Been pondering over it for centuries."

"What a terrible name."

"It's better than *Chai Karan*. For heaven's sake, you couldn't settle for just one name, had to give yourself *two—*"

"If I might remind the pair of you," Lask said, growing irritated with them, "The Mirror of Dùmsaro is free."

"There is no rush," Chai Karan replied, "So long as I am in the Void, time has stopped in Etheria."

"You're quite right, Lask," Gonamadé said, "Silly of us to be bantering about when there's real work to be done. Let's be off, shall we?" He reached down and plucked the second gold key from the bandolier, holding it aloft.

Everything lurched again, and suddenly all the colors, sounds and smells of the Great Hall came rushing back to assault their senses. Lask found himself standing exactly where he had been beside Chai Karan, only this time, Gonamadé stood on his opposite side. King Lavancer started, as the other Ancient seemed to appear out of nowhere.

"Ah, High King," said Gonamadé, bending into a

sweeping bow, "Ancient Gateway, at your service, sire!"

"Hello," Lavancer said, eyeing the newcomer.

"I'll explain later," Lask told him.

"Come," said Chai Karan, "The Mirror will surely go after the Dragons, as that was its intended purpose. We must warn Scoarin and her Kyn."

As Scoarin and many of the Dragons had been attending the festivities, they went out into the courtyard in search of her, but the yard and the fields beyond the walls were devoid of dragons. At the first word the Mirror of Dùmsaro was free, they had all taken to the skies, fleeing back to their lairs.

"Her lair is not far," Lask said. "We can be there within the hour."

Chapter Two

Lavancer stayed behind to explain the situation to the guests at the castle and to the United, while Lask and Myranda rode through the Carthonian alongside Chai Karan. The Gateway flew through the dark sky above them, wings keeping pace with their horses. They were approaching the river when a terrible roar rang through the trees.

They kicked their horses even faster, closing the distance to the caverns by the riverbank. Chai Karan and the Gateway were already rushing inside, Lask and Myranda dismounting to follow close behind them.

The cavern was lit by a sinister green light. The Mirror stood in the central chamber, tendrils of its magic having ensnared the dragon leader. Scoarin writhed on the floor, as if in agony, roaring and screaming, but could not twist free of the glowing green cords that had caught her. Her son, Calliban was clawing at the Mirror, but could not leave a scratch on it.

"Stay back, Calliban!" Scoarin was crying.

The Ancients rushed into the cavern. Scoarin caught sight of them and Lask coming in after them.

"Vatron is my successor!" she shouted to them.

"Do something!" Lask snapped at the Ancients.

They had already set upon the Mirror, pressing themselves in against the back of it, grimacing as if struggling against some great weight, golden sparks and wisps of magic pouring off of them onto the Mirror. Lask could only look on, helpless, watching Scoarin struggle in her bonds, her screaming seeming to echo inside both the cavern and his own head. Her golden body twisted and flailed, wings straining against the magic that held her.

"Calliban," she cried, "Calliban, my son—"

There was a rumbling crack and a blinding flash of green light. When it cleared and Lask looked to the center of the cavern again, Scoarin was gone.

"No!" roared Calliban, flinging himself at the place where she had lain. "Mata! No!"

Green light was beginning to spill anew from the Mirror, but the Ancients braced themselves against it and Chai Karan roared. There was a flash of their own power and the Mirror was caught in golden cords of their magic, unable to release its evil further. Lask swept around in front of it, demanding,

"Where is Scoarin?"

The face in the Mirror just gave a crooked, silent, smirk.

"*Where is she?*" Lask snarled at it.

"Gone," grunted the Gateway from behind the Mirror. "We cannot help her now—"

"What are you—?"

"There's not much time," said the Gateway. "We cannot hold it like this very long. You must go, fly with Calliban, to the Finistriel Forest. Find the wizard Socadan."

"I'm not leaving here," growled Calliban, voice harsh in his grief.

"Please, Calliban," the Gateway told him, "You are the fastest. You know where to find him. Go, else this shall be the fate of all your kind."

The black dragon rose from his place crouched on the cavern floor and went, grim and silent, to help Lask and Myranda up onto his back, walking out of the caverns to launch himself into the sky.

Calliban had always been the fastest flyer of the dragons, but his wings pumped even faster in his distress, flinging them across the night sky high above the treetops, out over the open fields and the castle, and on to the Finistriel beyond.

"Calliban," Lask started, pressing a hand against the dragon's scaly neck. The dragon's crazed pace concerned him, but before he could say more, Calliban snarled,

"Say nothing, I beg you, sir."

Lask could hear the tears threatening to break the dragon's voice, and so complied, settling back and falling silent. The dragon soared over the Finistriel, and banked southward over the trees for perhaps a half an hour, until he finally tucked his wings to dive into a clearing there.

The place was in shambles. The clearing was illuminated by the light of the moon and by its silver light, Lask could see the yard was completely under siege by briars and other prickly plant life, though it was the house that held his attention. The cottage was a pathetic sight. The small front porch sat crooked, one of the supports having collapsed. One of the windows was broken and the rest were coated with a thick film of dust. The roof looked sagged and was sure to leak in numerous places.

"Are you sure this is the right place, Calliban?" Myranda asked.

The young dragon sniffed and nodded.

"Come on," Lask said, resigned.

He slid down from the dragon's back, offering a hand up to help Myranda down, then picked his way across the yard, tugging his cloak from the grasp of one of the many briars only for the hem of his coat to get stuck on another. Myranda was having an equally difficult time, her dress snagging on the bushes until she finally just gave up and hefted it up around her waist in favor of doing an undignified trample through the yard.

Lask went up the three stairs, the steps bowing and creaking under his weight, and approached the grime-caked door, hearing Myranda come up behind him. He knocked, wondering if he might inadvertently cause the door to fall in by doing so. For a moment, there was silence, then came the sound of scuffling inside. A small panel slid back in the middle of the door and a beady blue eye glared out.

"Who are you?" a voice demanded. "What do you want?"

"I am Lask Somadar, and this is my wife, Myranda," Lask replied, wondering how anyone could *not* recognize him from his distinctive appearance.

"And? What do you want?"

Lask exchanged a glance with Myranda and replied, "The Mirror of Dùmsaro is free, and—"

"*What*?" squawked the voice.

The door was wrenched open, a cloud of dust issuing out, which made both Lask and Myranda cough. A tiny old man scurried out and Lask looked down at him, stunned.

He stood only as high as Lask's waist, and was by far the oldest-looking Etherian Lask had ever seen. The man was hunched, scuttling about with a knobby cane. Wiry tufts of grey hair stuck out from under a moth-eaten hat and his wrinkled body was covered in an equally shabby robe, repaired half-heartedly with unmatched patches. He looked up with a crinkled face and hooked nose, with one piercing blue eye, the other obscured by a milky cataract.

"You of all people should know it's rude to stare," he groused and stamped his cane down on Lask's foot. "This is what too much magic will do to a man!"

Lask yelped and started in spite of himself, looking down at the old man, shocked and indignant.

"What's all this about the Mirror being loose then? Eh?" demanded the old wizard.

"The Mirror escaped," Calliban growled from out in the yard, "And took my mother!"

"Good heavens," said Socadan, just noticing the dragon. "I'm terribly sorry, Calliban."

"Time and the Gateway are holding it for now," Lask said, "But they cannot hold it for long and have asked for your help."

"Of course they have," grumbled the old man. "I'm the only one left who'd be any use against it, since the First all up and died. Just grand of them, wouldn't you say?"

He kept muttering, walking back into the house, leaving the door open. Lask guessed they were supposed to follow him. Inside, the house was in the same state as the exterior. Ramshackle and covered in dust, Lask wondered how anyone could live in it. The rooms were filled with what had once been nice furniture, but it had long since been worn threadbare and moth-eaten. The fireplace was black with soot and grime, and it seemed that every available space in the house had been packed tight with books, measuring instruments and jars of plants, bones, and other relics. The floor groaned under their weight as they walked, and in places the floorboards were broken and fallen away entirely. Myranda grabbed the back of Lask's cloak to keep him from stepping into one such hole.

They followed Socadan into one of the back rooms, where several counters stood. The walls were lined with shelves, filled with books, scrolls, and things that Lask could not decide just *what* they were.

"Now you two stay put and don't touch anything," said Socadan. "I'll get the necessary things to bind the Mirror more permanently." He kept speaking, but his voice fell away into an incomprehensible grumble and Lask decided he was just talking to himself at that point.

The old man scuttled around the room like a crab in the shallows, gathering books and jars. Lask and Myranda couldn't help but look over the shelves while he worked. There were jars of teeth and scales and hair. There were bottles of what looked like blood and some blue ooze that

Lask didn't particularly want to know what it was.

There were bones of different creatures among the shelves and small cages housing beetles and mice and other small animals. Dried herbs hung from the ceiling, though a few had fallen to the floor, adding to the debris that Socadan waded through without a thought. Myranda moved closer to one of the shelves, studying something, while Lask inspected what looked like a dried up hand. He looked away to something else, only to be greeted by bowlful of small eyeballs.

Suddenly, Myranda yelped and Lask looked to see that she had opened a box and a plant vine had shot out and wrapped around her wrist. She clawed at the thick vine and Lask joined her, but to no avail.

"Give me that!" Socadan exclaimed, snatching the box. The old man yanked the plant from Myranda's arm and shoved it back in the box (Lask could have sworn he heard the plant squeal) and closed the lid. "I said don't touch anything!"

Socadan glared at Myranda and shuffled back to the counter. Lask and Myranda exchanged glances as she rubbed her wrist, certain a bruise would soon be appearing, and made sure to keep a safe distance from the shelves.

Lask moved around her to the next shelf and looked over the books there, skeptical about some of the titles:

'The Magical Art of Burning Beetles', 'The Science of Star Reading', 'Ancients and What They Don't Want You to Know.' Myranda snickered and nudged him, pointing to a particularly amusing title: *'Water Magicks: Floaters and Sinkers.'* Lask gave an amused snort.

"What's so funny over there?" demanded Socadan.

"Nothing," Lask replied.

"Good. Make yourselves useful. Lady, there's a box of phoenix feathers over there. Pick me out the longest of them, would you? And you, red eyes, can grind me up three handfuls of those black beetles there." He pointed to a jar on one of the shelves.

Lask went to the indicated shelf and looked in the corked jars until he found the proper one. Locating a carved wooden bowl to work in, he measured out a few handfuls as he had been instructed and took up a large wooden spoon to grind them with. He paused for a moment, looking down at the glittering black beetles, which were all shriveled and dead in the bottom of the bowl. He started crushing them, trying not to be disgusted at the sickening crunch made with each press of the spoon.

As he worked, Lask became aware of an odd sensation in the back of his mind. It was a gnawing sense of unease, bewilderment, and fear. Lask paused, confused, and suddenly realized the emotions did not belong to him. An image flashed in his mind of the Gateway struggling to keep a hold on the Mirror alongside Chai Karan.

Myranda sneezed, breaking his concentration, and Lask glanced over to see that she had blown the dust off of a thin, wooden box. She looked through it, then withdrew a long red and gold feather that shimmered in the dim candlelight. Turning back to his task, Lask continued to crush up the beetles, their dried legs beginning to stick to the bottom of the spoon. Every now and then, he would stop and scrape them off, but they just kept sticking. Socadan came over and shoved Lask out of the way to rummage in a cabinet under the counter.

"I just need one more thing," the wizard muttered, "But it's gotten away from me somehow."

"What is it?" Lask inquired.

"This bowl I have. A small wooden one, carved around the edge with Eurydicen leaves. It's an Anointing bowl; used for all kinds of sacred and pure magics."

Lask cast a guilty, hesitant glance down at the bowl he held, the squashed, smeared dust of the beetles piled in the bottom, a few little legs sticking up out of the heap. Socadan stood up then and caught sight of it.

"You've gone and smushed beetles all in my Anointing bowl!"

"I didn't know—"

"Give me that, you ill-colored idiot!"

Socadan snatched the bowl from him, ignoring

Lask's indignant huff. Myranda snickered from behind him. Lask glared down at Socadan, watching the wizard dump the beetle-debris into another jar and rub the bowl clean with his sleeve, and thought that surely he would have had a few words for the wizard if the circumstances were not so dire.

"Now come on!" groused Socadan hobbling back toward the front door, grabbing the phoenix feather from Myranda as he passed. "Don't have all night!"

Chapter Three

When they arrived back at Scoarin's layer, Socadan leapt down from Calliban's back, surprisingly spry for his condition. Lask and Myranda followed him inside to where the two Ancients still stood braced against the Mirror, holding it fast with their magic. The wizard laid out his supplies and took up the bowl and knife, saying,

"Calliban, might I trouble you for a bit of blood?"

Calliban offered his arm and the wizard pried up one of his scales, letting the dragon's blood drip off into the bowl. When he had enough, he wiped off the knife and turned to Lask, saying,

"And we certainly can't pass up a bit of Somadar blood. Let's have it then."

Lask complied, rolling back his sleeve to let Socadan prick a vein in his arm, wondering why the wizard was so much politer to Calliban. Once he'd collected the blood,

Socadan poured in the ground beetles and the contents of three different phials he'd brought. Taking up a shard of unicorn horn, he stirred up the mixture, then flicked a few drops onto the back of the Mirror. They sizzled where they fell and Lask heard the face of the Mirror snarl from the other side. Ignoring it, Socadan took up the phoenix feather, dipping the plume into the bowl, and used it to draw out a strange symbol on the floor, saying,

"Lecere Salectùs de Dùmsaro eladilergobòn actho brùnòan é énvocàntiel ìaton."

He worked his way in a slow circle around the Mirror, drawing out seven shapes, repeating his words with each glyph. With each symbol, it was as if the air thickened. Lask thought he felt it moving over his skin, though there was no wind, and it seemed to crackle with gathering energy. When Socadan had made a complete circle, he raised his hands, and he and the Ancients spoke together,

"Lecere Salectùs de Dùmsaro eladilergobòn actho brùnòan sié énvocàntiel ìaton. Lecere vé elcapébòn ì velo locùriauno!" [2]

Socadan brought his hands together in a sharp clap and there was a flash of golden light. When it subsided, the circle of symbols glowed red, coils of gold magic

---

[2] "Let the Mirror of Dùmsaro be bound by the power we now summon. Let it be captured in this place!"

weaving between them, connecting them into a solid circle. The Mirror itself was bound in golden cords of light. The Ancients stepped back, cautious, then stepped out of the circle.

"It is done," said Time.

"Where is Scoarin?" Lask asked. "What has become of her?"

"I cannot say," Chai Karan replied.

"Is she—?"

"She is not dead, no," said the Ancient. Calliban raised his head from nearby, only to drop it back down again when Time finished, "But she will never return."

"What does that mean?" Lask asked.

"She has been magically banished to Earth, lost somewhere in that vast world at some point in its history. We will never know when nor where."

"Surely there is some way to track her, to search for her—"

"There is not," Chai Karan said. "We tried long ago when the Mirror was first made, but it was made too well for its purpose. I fear that Scoarin is now lost to us forever."

Gonamadé had moved over to Calliban, laying a furry hand on the dragon's head, but Calliban just snorted sparks at him, pulling his head away and slinking back into the darkness of the cave. The Gateway watched him go, then trudged outside away from everyone.

"Now what?" Lask asked of Socadan and Chai Karan.

"It is very late. We will address the United in the morning," said the Ancient. "Socadan, the Gateway and I will take shifts watching the Mirror, although we really don't need to with that spell. We will come to the castle in the morning and decide what to do from there."

Lask nodded and left them for the night. As he and Myranda went out of the cave, Lask spotted the Gateway sitting on a low rock down by the river.

"I'd like a word with him before we go," Lask said. "I won't be long."

Myranda nodded and went to wait by their horses. Lask went down toward the river, walking up behind the Gateway.

"Ancient?" he ventured.

"Oh for heaven's sake, Lask, I lived inside you for four hundred years. I think that puts us on a first name basis."

"Gonamadé?"

"Yes?" said the Ancient, turning to face him with a toothy smile. Lask was surprised at how happy he could look when he had seemed so disheartened only moments before.

Lask sat down beside him and Gonamadé scooted over a bit to make more room on the rock.

"Ever since," Lask paused, trying to find the right phrasing, "Since you separated from me, I've had this odd sort of feeling. I am somehow *aware* of you. I can distinctly feel your emotions, your thoughts, somehow—"

Yes, of course you can, came the Gateway's voice, but the Ancient had not spoken. Lask realized he had heard the voice in his own mind.

"I can hear your thoughts?" he asked.

When I want you to, came the reply.

Can you hear mine? Lask wondered, not sure how to communicate with thoughts.

Yes. When you want me to, I can.

Will it always be like this?

What do you mean? inquired the Gateway.

"What if I don't want you in my thoughts?" Lask asked, deciding he preferred speaking aloud.

"Afraid there's no getting around it," Gonamadé replied. "You were my host; that means I remain connected to your body on some level until you die. I've never separated from a host while he was still living, so I admit, it's a new sensation for me as well. I quite like it, I think. It gives a delightful little tingle to the back of the mind."

Lask wasn't sure he shared the Ancient's enthusiasm.

"Stop that brooding," said the Gateway.

Lask glanced over at him, thinking he most certainly did not like the Ancient being able to feel whatever emotions were stirring in him at a given moment.

"I know for you, you are just meeting me," Gonamadé said, "But try to remember I've known *you* for centuries. I know practically everything there is to know about you, seen you in every possible state—"

"That is what worries me," Lask muttered, not liking the fact that every moment of his adult life had been witnessed by someone else, and an Ancient no less.

"Nonsense. You are a perfectly decent man and natural human being. I've shared the bodies of five different creatures; I know all about the ups, downs, ins and outs of life, the needs, the delights, the sufferings. You've nothing to be ashamed of. I don't know exactly how I think of you—perhaps as a son, or a brother— all I know is that I like you a great deal and I hope you will like me too." There was that toothy grin again.

Lask just watched him, wary.

"Think of me as your confidant," said the Ancient. "I know everything about you, but you can rest assured that I'm not going to tell another soul about anything you've done in private, not that any of it should embarrass you or damage your reputation. You are a fine fellow, you know."

"But if you've lived in me for so long," Lask said, "That means you not only know me, but you know my wife—"

"And your son, daughter-in-law, granddaughter,

brother, Forge. Yes, I know all of them as well as you do. If you don't mind, I like to think of myself as part of your family."

Lask said nothing. The Gateway looked back at him, looking a bit forlorn at the fact Lask didn't seem to be as enthused about their meeting, and Lask couldn't help but feel a little sorry for him.

"You saved my life, did you?" he asked after a moment.

The Gateway nodded.

"Thank you."

"You're very welcome," said the Ancient. He nudged him with a wing. "And I shall do my best to save it as many times as I can in the future."

Chapter Four

When morning came, Lask rose before the sun (much to Myranda's frustration) and left to seek out Vatron before the council met. Vatron was dozing on the outskirts of the United's camp, though not all of the dragons had returned yet. Lask approached the sleeping dragon. The growing light of dawn glinted faintly on her golden scales. Lask put a hand on her head.

"Vatron."

She snorted a puff of smoke, making Lask cough, and stirred at his touch. She blinked sleepy blue eyes at him.

"What is it?" she asked. "Is the Mirror—?"

"It's been contained for now," Lask replied, "But that's not exactly what I need to talk to you about."

He folded his legs to sit down beside her head and Vatron sat up a bit, curling her tail around herself.

"I fear I bring very bad news," Lask said. "We were

not able to find the Mirror in time. We were on our way to Scoarin's lair when it appeared there." He paused and glanced up at Vatron's concerned face. "Scoarin is gone."

"What do you mean?" said Vatron, shaking her head.

"She is not dead, say the Ancients," Lask replied, "But the Mirror's magic threw her into an unknown place and time on Earth and the Ancients say there is nothing any of us can do to help her. She is lost to us."

Vatron turned her head away, looking toward the sunrise, silent.

"Before she disappeared," Lask told her, "She named you as her successor as Leader of the Dragon Kyn."

Vatron's head tilted toward the ground.

"Will you accept it?" Lask inquired.

"Of course," Vatron murmured, "Scoarin wanted it to be that way if anything ever happened to her. I just never thought..." She paused and sniffed, turning her head away again. "She was the closest friend I ever had. Indeed, I have long thought of her as a sister."

Lask laid a hand on her scaly foreleg.

"And poor Calliban," said Vatron. "He has lost both his parents in only a month's time." She shook her head. "He's old enough to be on his own, certainly, but that cave will surely feel so empty now."

Lask sighed and nodded.

"The Ancients and I must address the council this

morning," he said, "But I wanted you to know first."

"Thank you." She wrapped a wing around him and was silent for a moment, then gave a slow nod. "I will tell the rest of the Kyn after the meeting. No doubt they will wish to do something to honor her."

Chapter Five

When Lask approached the gathering council, he saw they were all looking at Gonamadé with wary, skeptical looks. The Gateway was sitting among them, smiling, letting them conduct their inspection of him, and Lask could sense that he was at ease even under so much scrutiny. Chai Karan was there with him, head held high with his usual air of disdain.

"Before we begin," Lask said, coming to sit down with them, "I should introduce Gonamadé, the Ancient Gateway."

"I thought your host was a fairy," Julius said to the Ancient, suspicious.

"Oh, yes, Tarquinius," Gonamadé replied, "But he's been dead for some time now. I've been residing in Lask for the past four hundred years or so."

The councilors all glanced down to Lask, some looking amused, others stunned.

"I'll bet that was interesting," Julius remarked with a smirk. He glanced to the Ancient. "You must know everything there is to know, then."

"I do indeed," Gonamadé replied with a proud grin. "Sir Lask Maveran Somadar, born on the 21st of Warkila in the 208th Year of the Fourth Age to—"

"Gateway," Lask said with a pointed look.

Gonamadé looked guilty.

"*Maveran*?" Ossifer echoed.

"Yes, didn't you know?" said Gonamadé. "His parents hated each other by the time he was born and couldn't agree on what to name him. Luke wanted to name him Lask, of course, but Sasha wanted to name him after her grandfather, so they ended up just giving him both. He doesn't like people to know, since not many people have second names, and he thinks it makes him sound like some sort of snobbish—"

"*Gateway,*" Lask said again, giving him a look that promised pain would be in short order if the Ancient continued.

"Right," said Gonamadé. "Sorry." He waited til Lask looked away, then whispered to Rosecca, "Also loves strawberries."

"Do the Ancients know what we must do to destroy the Mirror?" Lask asked of Chai Karan.

"Yes," Time replied. "In order to break the Mirror, we will need to summon the Spirit who helped create it."

"A Zpirit?" said the Moranter leader, Asmodeus, looking wary.

"Yes," answered Chai Karan. "When the Dragons came to Etheria, they were followed by a mortal man who hated them, one called Sirezo. He wished to find a way to send the Dragons back to Earth so that they could be fully exterminated. To do so, he called on a dark Spirit, a Merrus by the name of Lothanvar. It was with the Merrus's help he created the Mirror of Dùmsaro. So long as Lothanvar exists in this world, his power will sustain the Mirror and make it unbreakable. To destroy the Mirror, we must first destroy Lothanvar."

"And how do we do that?" asked Sutonius, fanning his orange wings in the morning light.

"We must summon him, bind him, and condemn him," Chai Karan replied. "There are two types of Spirits, as many of you may know: the Terwini, good Spirits bound for Heaven, but who are kept here by unfinished work or unresolved problems, and the Merrui, wicked spirits bound for Hell, remaining in Etheria because they were never brought to justice during their lives. Lothanvar is the oldest Merrus left in Etheria, and therefore the most powerful. He is the Dùmsaro, the "king" Merrus, if you will. It will not be easy to bind him and banish him to Hell where he belongs."

"But we *can* do it?" pressed Ossifer.

"Yes. With the Gateway's help to control the Gate to Hell, and with all of your help to gather what we need to summon and bind him, I believe we can."

"And what do you need us to gather?" asked the centauress, Airda.

There was the sound of rustling as the Gateway pulled a folded paper out of his robe. He cleared his throat and read,

"Three diamonds, seven drops of mermaid blood, one sea serpent scale, one breath of Time, the reflection of Mystery, one eye from the Hydra King, one golden butterfly from the High Peaks, the light of Autrial, and one phial of water from the Spring of Life."

The council was silent and the Gateway glanced around at all the sets of wide eyes looking back at him.

"Are you mad?" asked Julius after a moment. "We don't even know where half those things are!"

"Then we shall have to find them, won't we?" replied the Gateway with a grin. "The castle library has extensive Ancient Etherian texts, I am sure with the right amount of research, we can find them all."

"We are warriors, not scholars," groused the centaur Polian.

"There is a female among my griffins," said Ossifer,

"Marjusina, who is one of the most prominent experts on the Ancient Etherian tongue in the kingdom. I'm sure she would be glad to help you."

"See?" said the Gateway. "That's a start!"

"I have a cousin," Sutonius added, "Named Montevale, who runs a shipping business out of Arajei. He has many contacts among sailors and others on the coast. Perhaps he could help us procure the mermaid blood and sea serpent scale."

"Excellent!"

"I could easily provide three diamonds from my hoard," offered Vatron.

"I have had *some* contact with the Hydra King," Julius said, almost reluctant. "I'll go to him and see what I can arrange."

"And I can go to the High Peaks and search," said Ossifer. "Surely someone knows where to find these golden butterflies."

"Very good," Gonamadé replied, looking over the list. "We have Chai Karan here, so the breath of Time is already taken care of. As for the reflection of Mystery, I'm sure she will come to us once she knows of our task, so we need not worry about that yet. That leaves the light of Autrial, and the water from the Spring. Happy hunting, one and all!"

Chapter Six

Lask could see the excited grin on the griffin's face. He had accompanied Marjusina to the library to help her search for information. She was not a large griffin; the top of her head was about level with Lask's or little shorter. Her most notable feature was her silky silver coat and feathers. It was a somehow rich hue and had a vibrant sheen in the light. Around her neck she carried a small leather satchel. Her bright blue eyes were eager to start hunting the shelves. Lask nodded to the Archiver at the front desk, a fellow nobleman by the name of Faileas Sìrodar.

"Chai Karan is already here," said the Sìrodar, "I've just started the other librarians pulling things for you."

"Thank you," Lask replied.

Marjusina went bounding back through the library toward the Ancient Etherian section.

The library of the castle was the largest library in the

kingdom, its only rival the library of Arajei, though the castle boasted a much larger collection of ancient books and scrolls. It was an enormous chamber, occupying much of the upper levels of the castle. There were rows upon rows of shelves, and the walls were lined floor to ceiling with books. The second floor of the library consisted of two curving mezzanines, on opposing corners of the chamber, which were connected by an arched bridge that soared above the main floor. As they made their way to the back, Lask spotted Chai Karan clopping along the arc of the bridge. He looked over the rail at them, but continued on, paying them no further attention.

Marjusina went to the backmost corner, where she set about looking over the books the librarians had already pulled. She picked up some of them and settled down in the floor nearby.

"What do you know of the Ancient Tongue?" she asked of Lask.

"Nothing, I'm afraid," Lask replied. "That's why I plan to make myself useful by assisting you."

"Oh, that won't do, sir. Could you fetch me some paper and ink please?" She spoke with a certain hesitation, and Lask supposed it *was* a rather unusual (and perhaps improper) request to make of the Somadar, but Lask gladly obliged, soon returning with the items.

She dipped the quill and scratched out a long line of

symbols on the paper. Lask had to marvel at the hands of griffins; they were much like humans', with four fingers and opposable thumbs, though they were thicker and furry and ended in sharp claws. When she had finished writing, she passed the paper up to him. Lask saw that she had written down all the letters of the Aetherian alphabet and their corresponding letters of the Common Tongue. There were also four lines of text in the ancient symbols. Marjusina tapped them with a grin.

"Would you be so kind as to find those titles for me?"

Lask obeyed, going away through the shelves, looking up at the section labels, which were thankfully written in the Common Tongue. It took a while, but Lask found the four titles, though there was one he was skeptical about. While he could not read the text inside, there were numerous illustrations and he knew the story well. When he returned to Marjusina, he was surprised to see that she had produced a small pair of magnifying spectacles and clipped them over her beak.

"My eyes turn two thousand next Memonsa," she explained.

"Just your eyes?" Lask teased.

"Yes, the traitors. I can still see at a distance just fine, but I fear I've begun to wear out my close vision from a millennium of reading tiny little text like this," she showed him the fine print in the book she was currently reading.

Lask noticed she'd been taking notes on another piece of paper and had a number of notations under the heading *The Spring of Life*. He handed the books over, but kept a hold on the one.

"This is a children's tale," he said.

"Yes, I know."

Lask gave her a dubious look.

"Don't you know the story, sir?" she asked.

"Yes. I think any Etherian would."

"Well then, you should know why it's relevant." She took it from him and opened the cover announcing, "The Adventure of Kaeron, a naughty little griffin who flew away from the roost of his family even though they told him not to." She turned to the first page, skimming it over. "Yes, there's what I want."

Lask watched her write down what she found in the text: *two hour flight from Griffin roost towards morning star.*

"Surely you're not thinking of taking directions from a children's story?" Lask said.

"Why shouldn't we?" inquired Marjusina. She motioned at the other books. "They all say that it lies somewhere in the eastern end of the High Peaks. Kaeron went that direction."

"It's a *story*," Lask pressed.

"Do you know where it came from?" she asked, looking at him over her spectacles. "By your silence, I'd say not." She went back to the title page. "No author listed. It's a legend that's been around seemingly forever, told in countless books. But who was the first to tell the story?"

"I'm guessing you know?"

"Eralyn, the Ancient Life herself."

"Really?" asked Lask, suddenly intrigued.

"I'll wager she knows what she's talking about," said Marjusina with a satisfied smile. "And if I'm right, this early version will be the most accurate and may even tell us what's waiting for us there." She flipped through the pages. "Such a powerful place will have powerful magic guarding it, I'm sure." She stopped at a particular illustration, showing what looked like an emaciated wolf, but with longer legs and blank yellow eyes. "The Shrieker," said the griffin, "Capable of producing a scream so terrible it can kill you." She turned to another illustration. "A room full of keys and only one that fits the door." She came to another picture. "A horse of fire that will only stand down to a secret name." She turned the page again. "Then at last you'll come to the Spring."

"Where Kaeron fell in and drowned," Lask said. "That's why this story is told; as an incentive for children to listen to their parents and not go gallivanting off after adventure."

"True," Marjusina replied with a chuckle, "But the

waters, being so grieved at causing his death, took part of his spirit and created the griffin constellation in the night sky."

"Legend," Lask said. "How can water feel grief?"

"Don't ask me," answered Marjusina. "I suppose we'll have to see when we get there."

Lask had to smile at the griffin's spunk.

"Assuming this is correct," he said. "Isn't it too easy? If this is the way, then why has no one ever found it? Why don't people go there often? The only ones I've ever heard of going there are the First themselves."

"And you heard about them because they made it back," the griffin replied, tone ominous. "Many others have gone looking for it. None have returned." She paused, taking in his grim look, then grinned. "Which, personally, I take as an excellent sign! If people returned, never having found anything, we wouldn't have much hope. But since *no one's* come back, they must have found *something.*"

"And what will stop us from meeting the same fate?"

Marjusina chuckled and said,

"My dear Somadar, you can unite the races and defeat Vortearigan, but a little adventure has you worried? If something bad were going to happen to us there, I daresay the Ancients wouldn't have bothered asking for the water."

Chapter Seven

The First were exhausted, sitting in the field just beyond their bound adversary. The Mirror was bound in cords of golden magic, both from their power and the three Ancients. Lu`corian had still not caught his breath. The Mirror had somehow sucked him into its surface and the Ancients had just managed to get him out before Maléchian strangled him. Socadan picked himself up and he turned to Chai Karan asking,

"What now? How do we destroy it?"

"We cannot destroy it," Time replied.

Lu`corian seemed to bristle under these words.

"Everything of this world can be destroyed," the Protector replied, rising. "There must be a way, we just have to find it."

"You do not have the means."

"The *means*?" Lu`corian echoed. "We have shaped the

very world under our feet. We can call on the highest power, command any of this world's resources—"

"Not enough," Chai Karan said with a haughty sniff.

"What Chai Karan means," said Mystery, stepping between the two before Lu`corian could snarl a reply, "Is that the First are not the ones meant to destroy it. Indeed, perhaps you cannot gather everything needed for its destruction because it does not exist now."

"Then what are we supposed to do?" Lu`corian demanded. "I'm not about to let that thing stay in this kingdom."

"We can imprison it," said Famas, a sandy-haired man who was host to the Gateway. "With the First's magic and ours, and some help from Socadan, we can ensure it will not escape."

"And if someone frees it?" pressed Lu`corian. "Such a power could surely corrupt many and create great enemies to this kingdom."

"You're good at hiding things," said the Gateway. "I'm sure we can find a way to have it be lost in history."

"I don't like this," Lu`corian answered, shaking his head. "Such a wicked power should not be permitted to exist. We must find a way to rid the world of it—"

"It is not yet time for that," Chai Karan told him.

"That is not a good enough answer."

"Some things must come to pass—"

"That is *not* an answer!" Lu`corian shot back. "If that thing has the power to nearly kill *me,* imagine what it could do to an ordinary person. You have seen what it can do to the Dragons. I will not leave such a threat—"

"We cannot destroy it now. All things have their place and time. This is a burden for the son of your son's son, not you—"

"Your prophecies are useless! Are we so selfish to leave this to our children?"

"It is not a matter of ethics—"

"Then what is it, pray tell?"

"Things must come to pass in a way that means something," replied Chai Karan. "Otherwise the Plan—"

"The Plan can be changed—"

"Do not be ignorant and stubborn, Lu`corian. You know as well as I do that there are great things intended for this world. Would you argue with the One who made you?"

"Certainly wouldn't be the first time," Lu`corian growled.

"Insolence and arrogance! You—"

"And who are you to say what is intended for me or this world?"

"I will not debate this with you. We have not the means nor the place to destroy it and no amount of arguing with me will change that." Chai Karan snorted at him, then turned, cantering away across the field.

Lu`corian turned the opposite direction, storming away back to the castle. The other First let him go, but Mystery followed him. Lu`corian ignored her, sweeping across the courtyard and into the chapel. He walked up the center aisle, the light streaming through the stained glass, sending a spray of colors over his white skin, glinting in the white strands of his hair, as he went to take a seat in one of the pews. He heard footsteps behind him.

"Do not vex me, Ancient," he growled.

Mystery dismissed his cantankerous look and slid into the pew beside him. She reached out, brushing a hand over his white mane, smiling to herself as she found a few golden strands there. Lu`corian cast a dangerous scarlet glare at her, but Mystery paid him no mind, continuing to run her fingers through his hair, rubbing his neck in the process.

"Go on," she crooned. "You know you can."

Lu`corian gave an irritated sigh.

"Why should I not destroy the Mirror?"

Mystery smiled at him from under her hood and moved in closer to him. Lu`corian sat still, having become grudgingly accustomed to her playful advances over the years. Mystery put her arms around him, bringing her face in close to whisper in his ear,

"Your blood will save this land. He will bring all of

Etheria under one banner in a unity that will not have existed since the very first days of this kingdom. Together they shall face much darkness, perhaps even the ending of the world, but it is through that darkness their strength shall be forged. Without the Mirror to try them, their strength will be incomplete and so they risk absolute failure in the end. If you wish this land to be the paradise you have always envisioned, you must let the Mirror stay, for if there is no darkness, there can be no dawn."

She brushed a warm kiss over his cheek and sat back, taking his hand in her own. Lu`corian sat in silence for a moment. Mystery toyed with his hand, tracing the line of each of his long fingers, but Lu`corian paid her no mind. After a time, he nodded.

"Very well," he said, "I hope the future you see is indeed the one that comes to pass."

Chapter Eight

The young queen Atlanta did her best to look regal when Salazar came in, but it was not convincing. The Letian castle had been almost burned to the ground by Vortearigan just three weeks prior. The remaining stone walls were blackened beyond all hope of scrubbing clean, and while repairs were well underway, the throneroom was still a sorry sight. She sat on a plain chair amid scaffolding and modest draperies, and looked far more like a little girl playing dress up than a convincing monarch.

"I had thought you would be back sooner," she said as the Etherian ambassador approached her. She looked down her nose at his pale face, wondering why he did not bow when he entered.

"We needed time to gather more supplies. Vortearigan was defeated, and I thought it would not be fair to deprive the soldiers a day or two to savor the victory they had fought for," Salazar replied.

"So you've spent the week feasting and celebrating while we scrape for food and freeze because *your* enemy decided to come here as a diversion."

"We returned to Earth as soon as we were able," Salazar replied, patient. "The kingdom has been at war, resources are not as easy to gather in such a short amount of time, and you require a great deal to sustain your people during the repairs." He reached into his coat to produce a small box and passed it over to her. "I remembered how much you liked them."

Atlanta opened the lid to find the box full of her favorite purple candies, ones that Salazar had brought her from Etheria since she was a baby.

"I'm not a girl anymore," Atlanta replied.

Salazar did not let the skepticism show on his face. Atlanta was no older than his own daughter, and Ariana was only seventeen.

"I know you resent Etheria for what happened here," he said, "But—"

"I resent that father of yours most of all," Atlanta growled. "He just up and leaves us, leaves you here in his stead, promises to continue our dealings with Etheria, then lets that rebel walk right up to our castle. How can he call himself the Protector when he cannot even keep his enemy in his own kingdom?"

"I think you judge my father too harshly. Vortearigan had agreed to a truce, came through in the dead of night during the worst blizzard of the year. We could not have seen him then even if—"

"All you've ever done is make excuses for him," muttered Atlanta.

"I would like to remind you, your majesty," Salazar said, voice steady and even, "That though you have banished my father, he still sends supplies to your kingdom so that you might rebuild and feed your people. The Etherian Senate is fast losing patience with you, and it is only by my father's goodwill that your people have not starved. You should take care not to insult him further, or me for that matter. We have helped you far more than your mortal neighbors, and while there has been darkness to come from our kingdom to yours, we have made every effort to make things right."

"Your dealings with us are very one-sided," the queen replied. "You Immortals come and go in our world as you please, yet you will not allow one of us to visit yours. We are allowed only what you see fit to give us, and your kind consistently look down on us as lesser beings."

"I myself am half Kwynnish. When have I ever treated you poorly?"

"I don't mean just you or me. The Immortals as a whole treat us mortals as if we are expendable. You and your father have both killed mortals, and all this time you've treated us like children."

"What would you have me do?" asked Salazar. "I have already explained to you why the Senate does not wish the location of the Gate to be disclosed—"

"And you think that is fair? You can find us whenever you want, but we are not allowed to find you?"

"What do you want?" Salazar asked her, growing frustrated with the girl.

Atlanta glared at him.

"Do you even know?" he pressed.

Atlanta was silent. She wanted to tell him to get out, to take all the Immortals with him, and to stay in their own kingdom, but she could not deny that Letiana, for now, needed Etheria's support. If she banished him now, her people would go hungry, as it was still several weeks before anything would start to grow, and Kwynn, the mortal kingdom to the north, had not been as generous as she'd hoped.

"I know you are angry," said Salazar, "And grieving the loss of your family. I know too that you are scared of what the future will bring, and all of that is perfectly understandable. All I ask is that you do not do anything rash until you have had time to properly sort through and control those feelings."

Chapter Nine

Lask was wandering back through the camp when he caught sight of the Gateway sitting with Forge and Ossifer while Capperith was making lunch. The Ancient was strumming on a small harp, and as Lask came in closer, he could hear him singing,

"As I was journeying toward the hills,
I passed a maiden fair,
A-workin' in the spacious fields,
All the crows to scare.

I got down from me horse's back,
And helped her in her task,
We set a pumpkin on stick,
Carved with a frightful mask.

When we were done a-workin' hard,
We sat down on a rock,
In thanks she kissed me, pulled me down,
And sat down on me—"

"*Gateway*!" came an outraged roar from Chai Karan, who was trotting past. The drokamerdor had been ignoring him, but his ears perked up as he caught the words.

Forge and Capperith snickered like two boys and Lask himself had to laugh, both at Gonamadé, and the look of horror on Chai Karan's face. The Gateway looked over his shoulder, realizing that Lask was there.

"Enjoyed that, did you?" he inquired with a grin. "I know another about a milkmaid that's positively titillating—"

A fresh wave of snickering bubbled out of Forge, but Chai Karan just growled,

"*No*. You're an Ancient, show a little propriety." He shot a look at Lask, as if suggesting the Somadar do so as well.

Gonamadé waited until Chai Karan pranced away to make a face at Time's back, whiskers twitching as his tiger-like face scrunched up in mockery.

"Always such a killjoy," the Gateway muttered.

Lask patted his shoulder as he passed.

When he returned to his tent, Myranda was not

there. Deciding to take a few moments to rest in the quiet, he went over to the table, looking for a book he had brought from his personal library. He heard the tent flap open behind him.

"Darling, have you seen that book I brought with me?" he asked.

He felt a pair of arms wrap around him from behind, a hand rubbing over his chest.

"Myranda?" he said. "Is everything alright?" He reached up and took the hand on his chest and paused. "You are not Myranda."

He whirled, but there was no one behind him. He heard quiet, delicate laughter and spun back, looking for the source, and started. There was a figure sitting at the table across from him, leaned back in the chair. She was a slight, dainty woman, wrapped in a thick brown cloak with intricate gold stitching around the hem. The hood was drawn down over her face, but Lask could see red lips pull back into a smile in the shadows.

"Ancient Mystery?" he inquired.

"Hello, Lask," she said with a pleasant, fond tone in her voice.

She leaned forward onto the table and though he could not see her eyes, Lask knew she was inspecting him from head to toe. Apparently pleased with what she found, her smile widened.

"I've heard many things about you," she said, "But I must say, you're more handsome than I thought you'd be."

Lask arched a dark brow at her and Mystery gave a quiet, girlish laugh. She got up and circled him, running a hand along his shoulders as she passed behind him and squeezed the top of his arm, seeming pleased with the muscle she found under her fingers.

"Ancient," he growled.

"The Gateway always did have good taste in hosts," she remarked. "I knew the United would be needing my help with the magic, but I also think *you* will need a bit of help from me as well." She stood in front of him, hands going up to grasp the sides of her hood. "I have not let many people see me," she said. "I hope you'll understand what a gift it is."

Her slender hands pulled back the hood and Lask found himself looking down at one of the most beautiful faces he'd ever beheld. She had thick, wavy brown hair, and smooth, alabaster skin that looked as soft as flower petals. Her plump red lips smiled at him as she looked up, blinking endless green eyes at him, the color of summer grass.

"Speechless, I see," she crooned, pleased. "Nothing to say after looking upon the face of Mystery?"

"Why?" Lask asked.

She gave a broad, white-toothed smile and gave a

satisfied hum.

"My *favorite* question," she said, "Oh I *do* like you." She reached up brushing back a lock of his ebony hair that had fallen over his shoulder.

"Ancient," Lask hissed, warning.

"Hush," she crooned, placing a finger to his lips.

Lask was swept with a strange feeling. It was a cooling, soothing sensation, and he found that he was totally at ease with having the Ancient so near to him.

"Do not bewitch me," he said, but his voice was not forceful or at all convincing under the weight of her magic.

"Why not?" Mystery teased. She slipped her arms around his neck, pressing herself in close to him.

"Get off of me," Lask said, trying his best to sound serious, but his voice came out as a quiet murmur.

He knew it was wrong, that he should yank her arms off of him, throw her out of his tent, but as much as his mind was protesting, he found he simply could not move. Her magic had twined around him, enchanting and bewitching his senses.

"Stop it," he said, and this time his voice carried a growl to it as he struggled against her magic. "This is wholly inappropriate."

"That's what makes it so much fun," Mystery teased. She stood on tiptoe, tilting her head up so to whisper in his ear. "And you can't deny there *is* a pleasure in it."

"I am a married man," Lask replied, "And though you are beautiful, I cannot tolerate you near me like this."

Mystery pulled back a bit to pout at him. She ran a hand down his face, fingers trailing along the line of his jaw, and she tilted her face up toward him again, whispering on his lips,

"My name is Caledria. Do not forget."

She smiled and Lask could smell the sweet scent of her breath and feel the warmth radiating off her face, not even an inch from his.

The tent door opened and Myranda stopped short at the sight. Mystery yanked her hood back up . Lask felt her magic release him and he shoved her away.

"What the hell is this?" Myranda demanded.

"I didn't," Lask exclaimed, horrified, "She just—"

"I wasn't talking to *you,*" Myranda growled. She stormed up to Mystery, demanding, "How dare you?"

"I am an Ancient—"

"And I'm his *wife,*" Myranda snapped back. "Touch him again and we'll see just what you can live through." With that, she shoved the Ancient out of the tent, then rounded on Lask, "And *you*—"

"I didn't," Lask said, "She snuck in here, used her magic—"

"Convenient. Big fight you were putting up—"

"When have I ever given you reason to disbelieve me? She put some kind of spell on me. I couldn't move even though I wanted to."

Myranda looked at him and sighed, then went forward to wrap her arms around him.

"I know," she said. "I trust you. But these," she brought her head up to kiss his lips, "Are mine, and nobody else should be touching them."

"She didn't."

"She was going to."

"I don't know why she was acting that way," Lask said. He felt Myranda squeeze him tighter.

"She'd just better behave herself, Ancient or otherwise."

Chapter Ten

Patron had agreed to fly Sutonius down to Arajei, as the dragon's wings could propel them much faster than the fairy's and the dragon would need to return to her lair for the diamonds. She dropped the fairy off at the main gate, then flew off toward her home in the cliffs beyond the city.

Arajei was the largest city in Etheria. The city proper was surrounded by tall white walls, upon which flew banners bearing the crest of the Lévonsar, the city's landlord. Sutonius passed through the tall gate, taking the main road through the city. Arajei was built on several large hills right up next to the sea. As the fairy walked, he could catch a glimpse of the glittering ocean between the buildings. It was the largest port in Etheria, its harbor seeing the comings and goings of hundreds of ships each week.

The streets were crowded and noisy, ringing with the

calls of merchants, the clopping of hooves, and the rumble of wagon wheels. Arajei had the most diverse population of anywhere in the kingdom, and it had become even more so since the Uniting. It seemed that almost every race was represented on the streets. Griffins perched on the tops of buildings, taking in the hustle and bustle. Unicorns browsed over the open markets alongside fairies and centaurs. Sutonius passed a moranter who was bartering with a butcher, offering to help him dig an expansion for his cellar in exchange for some prime cuts of beef for the next week.

Everything was colorful; bright lengths of fabric draped the merchant stalls and hung in shop windows. Flowers grew in rows along either side of the street and blossomed on vines that climbed up the sides of the buildings. Even the buildings, with their pristine white stone, were painted with decorative motifs; flowers and fish and intricate knots and moons. The smell of baking bread and cooking fish wafted on the air. Feeling a bit cramped in the crowds, Sutonius flitted into the air to fly the rest of the way down to the harbor.

He made his way over the city, following the road down to the harbor, where he landed. He picked his way around busy sailors, and impatient merchants, skirting barrels and crates being loaded and unloaded, until he at last walked out onto the docks. He strode the length of the pier, all the way to where a long, sleek ship was docked. It was of dark wood, almost black, with silver-painted embellishments at the bow and stern. The dark blue sails were slack or tied down and the ship seemed to rock sleepily in the noontide sun. Sutonius caught sight of the captain about the same time the captain noticed him coming down the dock.

"Ahoy, cousin!" called the captain. He opened his shimmering wings and leapt over the side of the ship, flitting down to the dock.

He was tall for a fairy, perhaps six feet, with cerulean wings that were adorned with three pierced rings along each upper edge by his shoulders. He wore a long blue coat, with brass buttons and turned back sleeves. His coat was cinched with a weathered leather belt tied in a jaunty knot on one side. He walked in soft grey boots that were folded down at the knee and wore a gold medallion suspended on a leather cord around his neck. A blue hat with a white plume sat upon his head, casting shade over canny blue eyes set into a debonair face, framed in a few stray locks of dark brown hair that had fallen loose from the tie intended to hold them back.

"I hoped to find you at port here," Sutonius said, greeting his cousin with a shoulder-smacking hug.

"Won't be for long," Montevale replied. "That is if that damned fabric merchant I'm supposed to be taking ever shows up. What brings you to Arajei?"

"I was hoping you could help me with something," Sutonius replied. "Word might not have reached Arajei yet, but the Mirror of Dùmsaro has escaped. The Ancients and the United must gather the necessary things in order to perform the magic to vanquish it."

"What do you need?"

"Mermaid blood and a sea serpent scale."

"Mermaid blood will run very expensive if you try to buy it," Montevale replied. "But if you harvest it yourself, it will save you quite a sum. I've had some dealings with merfolk. I can tell you how to deal with them. As for the sea serpent scale, I know just the man. Come on."

He set off down the pier and Sutonius followed him.

"I ought to warn you," said Montevale, "Atabax is a bit eccentric and rough about the edges. He went off with the uncle of your commander all those years ago."

"Aborzen Somadàrsath?"

"Aye. Their vessel was sunk by the Sea Serpents. Atabax was the only survivor. A fishing boat found him drifting half dead on a bit of the wreckage days after the attack. He hasn't been quite right since."

Montevale led him to a tavern called the Silver Shanty within sight of the docks. He went inside, tipping his hat to the barmaid as he passed.

"Ahoy there, Montevale," called the tavern keeper.

"That'd be yer cousin ye've spoken of?"

"He is indeed," Montevale replied. "We're looking for Atabax, is he—?"

"What ye be wantin', Sea Wings?" came a gruff growl from the corner.

"Ah, there you are." Montevale made his way over to the corner and Sutonius followed him.

There was a man sitting at the table in the far corner, leaned back in his chair, boots propped up on the table. He pushed his hat up from over his face, revealing a weathered, scraggly countenance. He had a scruffy, greying beard that grew on his chin and regarded them with weary blue eyes beneath bushy brows.

"This is my cousin, Sutonius," Montevale explained. "He's on an errand for the United, looking for a sea serpent scale."

"Har har, well ye've come t'the right man." Atabax pulled his feet off the table, letting the chair fall back to all fours. "See, that ol' Aborzen carved off two fingers from the beasts that sank me ship. I got a good crack on the head, so didn't see most o'the fightin'. When I finally woke up, Aborzen was gone. I figure the beasts dragged him int'the deep with the ship. But those two fingers he'd chopped off were a'floatin' there in the waves aside me. I don't know why I kept 'em, but I suppose it be lucky fer ye that I did. Though o'course, seein' as they're so rare, I don't wish t'be partin' with 'em fer nothin'."

"Oh come on," scoffed Montevale. "The United saved the entire kingdom from Vortearigan. The least you could do is give them one scale when they need it."

"Charity won't be feedin' me belly nor buyin' canvas fer me ship," Atabax replied.

"The Lord Commander assumed there would need to be purchases made," Sutonius replied. He produced one of the small pouches of silver Lask had given him and offered it to the captain. "Will that do?"

"Aye, I reckon it will," Atabax replied inspecting the contents with a satisfied smile. "Follow me, lads."

He led the pair of fairies out of the tavern, down the street that ran parallel to the harbor and into a battered-looking residential building that overlooked the port. He trudged up the steps and produced a key, letting himself into a dusty little apartment, which looked in sore need of maintenance.

"Make yerselves at home. Have a seat. I'll be right back."

Sutonius started for one of the wobbly looking wooden chairs but Montevale shook his head with a warning look.

"Last time I tried to sit in one of those, I ended up on the floor in a matter of seconds. I think he takes a sort of twisted pleasure in abusing his visitors."

Atabax returned and set a wooden box on the table. He wiped the dust off the lid and opened it, waving Sutonius in closer. The fairy came to look over his shoulder, seeing a heap of scales and long knuckle bones in the bottom.

"Take yer pick. Take two if'n ye like, in case those Ancients botch it up the first time." He rasped an amused chuckle.

Sutonius selected the two largest scales and thanked the captain. He and Montevale went back out into the city and Montevale led him toward one of the markets.

"When dealing with merfolk, you will want to find one of the maids. They are generally more interested in the affairs of the land and are easier to bribe, though also quicker to use their magic on you. Your commander is proof of that; his poor great-grandsire learned that fact the hard way."

Sutonius nodded, for few did not know what had happened to Lu`corian. He had agreed to answer a mermaid's riddle, and she was so furious that he won, she cursed him by sapping the color out of him, giving him the snowy-pale skin and fearsome red eyes that had become an enduring characteristic of the Somadar line.

Montevale wandered among the merchant stalls, saying,

"You'll want to find a nice piece of jewelry to offer

her. I've found they're particularly partial to emeralds and amethysts. Be very kind and flattering, as if wooing a woman to your bed, but do not trust her for a moment. Once you've convinced her to let you take a bit of her blood, do it, and leave quickly. They have beautiful voices, but do *not* let them enrapture you."

Sutonius selected a necklace that Montevale assured him would be pleasing to a mermaid, then they wandered back to the docks.

"Looks like my merchant has finally arrived," Montevale remarked, spotting a scurrying, impatient figure on the pier by his ship. "Best be off while the tide is high."

"You should come to the north soon," Sutonius said. "Finistrì is lovely in the spring."

"It is indeed. My brother has been writing me, wanting me to visit for some time. I have several more runs to make into the bay and up river, but I have left a few weeks in the summer free, so that I might go visit him and my two lovely nieces."

"I should very much like to see you all then."

"I'm sure he'd be glad to see you. He always says he doesn't see you nearly often enough for living in the same city. Though I suppose no one sees much of you, always having to chase after Julius as you do."

"It's certainly a full time job."

"Aye, that it is. Though I wager there is no one more capable of dealing with him." Montevale clapped him on the shoulder and said, "If you walk about a mile up the shore, there are some rocks in the shallows. I have often espied mermaids there. No doubt you would find one there on such a fine day as this."

"Much obliged, cousin."

"Do take care of yourself. I worry about you." Montevale gave him a fond smile and tipped his hat, then went away down the pier to his ship.

Sutonius walked along the beach, through the silky white sands, just out of reach of the steady crystalline waves. As he passed out of sight of the city, he heard a sound on the breeze. As he continued, he found that it was singing; the beautiful, clear voice of a woman.

He found its source further up the shore, sunning on the rocks in the shallows. The top half of her was a bare-chested woman, with long, light brown hair that clung, wet, to her back. Her skin glittered with faint purplish spots along her shoulders and arms and around her waist. At her hips, her body became a long, purple-scaled fish tail, ending in two elegant fins that swirled lazily in the water. She caught sight of Sutonius and stopped her singing, sitting up a bit to regard him with deep blue eyes and her full lips pulled back into an inviting smile.

"Fairy, fairy," she called in a sing-song voice. "What a

pair we'd make, me of the sea and you of the air. What things we might do together!"

"Wondrous things, I'm sure," Sutonius replied, wading out into the water to approach the rock on which she lounged.

She reached out to him, trailing a wet finger along the side of his face.

"You are truly the beauty of the sea," Sutonius told her.

"Such a kind little butterfly," she said. Her eyes narrowed then and she growled, dangerous, "But I know no land-walker comes looking for us without wanting something." She put her finger under his chin and Sutonius felt her nail dig into his skin.

"Smart as well as beautiful," the fairy remarked. "It is true, I do need your help with something."

"I thought so," she hissed. "And what is it then?"

"We must do a bit of magic that requires a few drops of mermaid blood." He reached into his pocket to produce the necklace. "And I'd never ask such a favor without offering you something in return."

She eyed the necklace with a hungry sort of look, then pouted a bit.

"It will hurt, won't it?" she said.

"I will try to be careful," he promised.

The mermaid regarded him with a look Sutonius

couldn't quite read.

"Well, alright," she said, then took his face in her hands, "But only because you're such a handsome fellow."

She offered him her arm and Sutonius drew his knife, gently pricking one of the veins there. He heard the mermaid whimper and she looked at him with sad eyes. He collected a bit of her shimmering blue blood in a phial, then eased back, corking the phial and tucking it back into his coat. He held the necklace out to the mermaid.

"Fasten it on for me, will you?" she asked, turning to offer him her back, pulling her damp hair out of the way.

Sutonius complied, draping the necklace around her neck and fastening the clasp at the back. As soon as he had done so, the mermaid rolled off of the rock, knocking him backward into the water. The fairy surfaced, sputtering and the mermaid grabbed his head to clamp a fierce kiss on him. She tasted of brine and fish and Sutonius was left spitting and wrinkling his nose when she finally withdrew. She laughed, leaping away, giggling at him as she porpoised through the waves back out into the deep water.

Sutonius picked himself up, thoroughly soaked, and wiped his face off, the foul taste of her still clinging to his tongue. He slogged back to shore, deciding he should be grateful that was the worst she had done to him.

Chapter Eleven

Malachi was sitting outside on the balcony of the Sea Breeze Inn in Arajei, looking outward over the glittering water of the harbor in the distance between dozing in the late morning sunshine. He almost didn't know what to do with himself; he had become so accustomed to being alone or having manacles around his wrists, he felt rather lost.

For over four hundred years, he had been in exile on Earth for poisoning the High King Sendanten. In the past autumn, he had returned to Etheria and bargained his knowledge of Vortearigan in exchange for being allowed to stay. To his amazement, he had been able to prove himself to his brother Lask and had won his brother's forgiveness and favor.

It was that favor which had gotten Malachi an audience with the King, allowing him to offer a sincere apology for his past crimes, a sincerity that convinced Lavancer as truly as it had Lask. It was with the apology and Lask's counsel that the King had granted Malachi a conditional pardon, provided he did not stray into his old ways. The one condition came walking out onto the balcony with him.

"You haven't moved from that spot the whole time I've been out, have you?" inquired Ecthallia.

"No," Malachi admitted, not ashamed in the least.

Perhaps the greatest amazement for Malachi had come when he realized that someone could actually *want* to be around him. Lieutenant Ecthallia, originally charged with overseeing his guards, had soon developed an affection for him that Malachi could not understand but was nonetheless grateful for. As long as he remained under Ecthallia's supervision, he was able to travel and live as he pleased.

The lieutenant came to sit on the armrest of his chair, looking out toward the ocean, only to be pulled over into Malachi's lap. Her protests were unconvincing and she soon settled there against him.

"It is nice here, isn't it?" she said, resting her head on his shoulder.

"We could stay a little longer."

Ecthallia glanced over her shoulder at him and Malachi gave her that crafty grin she had come to adore. His green eyes flicked down to the street below.

"What is it?" she asked, shifting to follow his gaze. Her eyes were drawn to a pair of pumpkin-orange wings fanning on the street below. "Sutonius," she said, watching the fairy make his way up the street.

"He's headed this way. I'll wager he's looking for you."

Ecthallia made an irritated noise, watching Sutonius enter the inn below. She got up, straightening her clothes, and it wasn't long before there was a knock at the door. Malachi rose to answer it before she could reach it.

"You'd better not be here to say Lask changed his mind," Malachi said.

Ecthallia pushed him out of the way, saying,

"Don't mind him, Sutonius, I haven't yet had a chance to teach him any manners. Would you like to come in?" She paused. "Why are you wet?"

"Mermaid," the fairy replied. "I was here on an errand and offered to deliver a message to you. The Mirror of Dùmsaro has escaped and the United have reassembled. You are needed in the north. The Lord Commander wishes you to return as soon as you can."

"We'll leave this afternoon."

"I came with Vatron, who would be glad to carry you back to the north. We plan to leave in a few hours."

"We'll meet you at the main gate, then."

Sutonius nodded and bid them goodbye for the time

being.

"Always something, isn't it?" muttered Malachi as she shut the door. "Never a moment's peace."

"Not when you have the Protector's blood or you work for him," Ecthallia agreed. "Come, get your bag and pack."

Chapter Twelve

The air was cold so high up. Lask kept his cloak wrapped tight and found himself wishing he'd brought a pair of gloves; however, he was too preoccupied with the growing sick feeling in his stomach to worry about the cold. He and Myranda were hunkered down on Marjusina's back as the griffin flew them northward. Forge flew alongside them on a golden griffin named Messalo, who Marjusina had badgered into going with them since both Ossifer and Morpheus left earlier to seek out the golden butterflies.

With each stroke of the griffin's wings, Marjusina's body gave a lurch that made Lask's stomach tighten. It was not unlike being seasick. While he had flown on the backs of griffins before, Ossifer was considerably larger than Marjusina, and so did not have to work as hard to carry them. Marjusina insisted it was no trouble, but her smaller frame did make for a much bumpier flight.

They reached the city of Farisdon as the sun was setting. It was the third largest city in Etheria, situated on the banks of the huge Lake of Goltor. The streets were quiet in the deepening twilight as Lask and his companions walked through the city to an inn, where Lask secured them a few rooms for the night and paid for their supper.

While they were sitting in the common room, making a supper of baked fish and potatoes, Ossifer and Morpheus were on the other side of the city, asking about golden butterflies. The pair of griffins had not found much success that afternoon and were thinking of calling it a day, when a man came and tugged at the tip of Ossifer's wing to get his attention.

"I hear ye two have been a-lookin' for gold butterflies," he said.

"We have," Ossifer replied, "Do you know of them?"

"Not me, but I know one who would." He pointed down into an alleyway nearby. "There's a door down there. Ye'll find one named Androla there. She'll know about those butterflies ye seek."

"Thank you," Ossifer said.

The man nodded and disappeared down the darkening street.

"Looks awfully dark down there," Morpheus remarked, eyeing the alley. "Doesn't look like anyone lives there."

"It's the best lead we've gotten all day," Ossifer told his son, starting down the alley.

The griffins' keen eyes cut through the darkness, seeing dusty cobblestones and a few broken crates to one side. The door the man had spoken of was set into the side of what looked like an abandoned building. The door itself was splintery and worn.

"Could be a trap," Morpheus hissed, wary.

"What would be the point?" Ossifer replied, equally quiet, though he didn't know why. "We're not at war anymore and neither of us even brought anything that could be stolen." He reached out and knocked on the door. A voice answered almost immediately, seeming to come out of the walls and the door itself,

"What do you want?"

"We're looking for Androla," the griffin replied. "We were told she might be able to help us."

The door swung open.

"Come in," said the voice.

The two griffins went inside, finding themselves in a dim, musty room. It was cold inside, much colder than it had been in the alleyway. A thin blue rug covered the floor, and the furniture was all covered with a layer of undisturbed dust and grime. Several candles flared nearby, offering a bit of light. There was a woman there, with pale skin and dark hair. She had sorrowful green eyes rimmed in dark circles and was clad in a moth-eaten dress of faded blue. She could have been beautiful, but years of sadness and hardship seemed to have faded her away. She walked with uncharacteristic grace, almost floating over to them. Ossifer noticed she seemed to have a nervous habit of putting a hand to her belly.

"I am Androla," she told them. "What do you want?"

"We are seeking a golden butterfly. We were told you might know where to find them."

"So the United *are* trying to summon Lothanvar."

"How do you know that?" asked Ossifer, thinking word could not have spread that quickly.

"I know many things," Androla replied, "Particularly about Lothanvar and Spirits." She came in closer to them and Ossifer was suddenly wary.

Androla reached out to him, as if to touch his face, and her hand passed right through him. Ossifer's beak fell open and Morpheus scrambled for the door.

"I will not hurt you," said Androla, "I am a Terwinus, not like my wicked counterparts of the Merrui."

Morpheus stood still but watched her with a cautious golden eye.

"I know where to find your butterflies," she said, "And I will take you there."

Chapter Thirteen

Lask was awakened by the sound of a claw rapping on the door. Myranda gave a sleepy grunt of protest. Lask sat up, seeing the sky was still black outside, and went to the door, blinking bleary eyes at Marjusina who stood there.

"Good morning!" said the griffin with a broad smile. "Best be up. We must be at the Griffin Roost by sunup to follow the star properly."

"What time is it?" Lask groaned.

"About three hours or a little more before sunrise," replied the griffin, as if it were normal to be awake at such an ungodly hour. "We should leave ample time to fly to the Roost. Never know when there might be a head-wind."

Lask nodded and trudged back inside to get dressed. He and Myranda dragged themselves downstairs to find a groggy Forge sitting at a table with Marjusina, picking half-heartedly at a plate of breakfast. The maid brought plates for Lask and Myranda, and another for Messalo when he finally stumbled into the common room.

"About time," Marjusina remarked. "Always the last to arrive."

"A perfectly normal response to such a godforsaken hour of the morning," the gold griffin growled in reply. He tipped the plate up to his beak and slid the contents off with his long tongue, seeming to swallow the entire breakfast in a single gulp.

"Such manners," muttered Marjusina.

They set off into the dark sky, the griffins' eyes finding the landmarks below with ease. It was chilly in the still-dark air and Lask felt Myranda tuck her head in against his back, sheltering her face from the wind. It was about a two-hour flight to the Griffin Roost, and when they arrived, Messalo was grumbling that he could have slept for a whole extra hour. Marjusina paid him no mind, landing at the top of the Griffins' mountain to rest for a while and await the sunrise. Lask slid from her back and stood at the peak, Myranda coming to stand beside him. Lask put an arm around her shoulder, offering a bit more protection from the wind against his side under the folds of his cloak.

As the pale light began to kindle in the East, the sun appeared as a molten sliver on the horizon, beyond the sharp spires of the mountains. The air was clear; it was as if they looked into forever. The wind was crisp and cold but bore the sweet scent of early spring flowers. The sun began to paint everything in warm watercolor hues of rosy gold and Lask would have been content to stay on the mountaintop in the quiet, but Marjusina waved him over to where she had situated herself to take off from the peak.

The two griffins leapt off the mountain, their wings catching the wind to soar off into the glow of the sun. Lask found the bright glimmer of the Morning Star high in the northeastern sky, and the griffins seemed to steer a straight line toward it. It was quiet so high above the mountains; only the rustle of the griffins' feathers and the fluttering of the humans' cloaks broke the stillness of the morning. As the sun climbed higher, the star began to disappear and Marjusina and Messalo looked toward the ground, scanning for any sign of the entrance to the Spring. The star vanished as the sky began to cool into the blue of daytime.

"Maybe we've missed it," said Messalo. "Kaeron was just a little thing; perhaps he could not fly as far as we did in that amount of time."

"It has to be here," said Marjusina, circling, but they could see nothing.

They took Messalo's suggestion and began to backtrack, flying slowly, studying the mountains below. Everything looked the same, the pale, purplish stone of the mountainsides, white snowcaps, glistening streams far below.

"There!" exclaimed Marjusina pointing.

She tucked her wings and swooped down, Lask's fingers tightening in her hackles at the sudden dive. He felt like he'd left his stomach somewhere a few hundred feet above, but soon saw the source of her excitement. In the midst of the pale stones of the mountainside, there was a single, large black rock. Marjusina braced herself against it and it rolled to the side with surprising ease.

"A rock that big shouldn't—"

"It's a magical entrance," Marjusina said, cutting off Forge's wondering, "It's here only to disguise, not keep people out. Those magics are waiting inside."

"Wonderful," muttered Messalo.

Marjusina set off down the steps into the passageway below. The others followed her, Messalo bringing up the rear. As soon as the golden griffin had passed, the boulder snapped back into place with surprising speed. Messalo yelped and leaped for it, but was too slow. He tried to shove it back out of the way, but it would not budge.

"Now we're trapped," he whined.

"As we should be," Marjusina replied, "The same thing happened to Kaeron. Besides, we won't be needing to go that way again."

"What about escape?" whimpered the other griffin.

"Oh don't be a hatchling," retorted Marjusina with a dismissive flick of her tail.

The passage was lit by a faint silver light, an ancient magic left to illuminate the way. Marjusina followed the corridor's winding route, having to tuck her wings in tight against her body in the narrow places. The others followed her, Messalo muttering under his breath at the back. They came to an archway that opened into a wide cavern.

"The Shrieker's chamber," said Marjusina, passing inside.

Lask and the others filed in behind her, wary and watchful, but there was no sign of the creature. There was a pedestal at the center of the room. Lask approached it, hearing Messalo say,

"Maybe it's gone."

The pedestal hosted a deep stone bowl, filled with dark green-tinted water. Around the edge of the bowl were Ancient Etherian symbols.

"Marjusina," Lask called.

"Strange," she said, walking across the room to the pedestal, "I wonder where it is? It was waiting for Kaeron."

As she approached the pedestal, a gust of wind blew

through the chamber, rippling the dark water and splashing several drops onto the floor. Where the droplets fell, something began to rise out of the stone. It twisted and shifted, forming into the shape of an enormous black wolf. It was impossibly skinny, with too-long legs that bent and crouched. Tufts of purple hair grew from its joints, and a long lion-like tail swung back and forth behind it. Its ears flattened and it looked at them with glinting yellow eyes that had no pupils.

"Why do you dare to trespass here?" it snarled.

"We come seeking the Spring of Life," Lask replied.

"To pass you must pay the boon."

"The boon?" echoed Marjusina, not recalling such a price from the story.

"I will let you pass if I might dine on one of you," the Shrieker replied.

"None of us shall feed you," Lask answered. He drew his sword from his shoulder. "Let us pass."

"If you will not pay the boon, then you will die," it answered.

It threw back its head and let out a terrible cry. It was deafening, a shrill shriek of maddening pitch, seeming to pierce through any sensible thought into the very core of the soul. Lask reacted on instinct, lashing out at it, slicing it across the shoulder. The Shrieker's cry was cut off as it yelped. Black smoke poured from the wound, and Lask doubted it would die by any normal means. It threw back its head again, but Lask swung at it once more to keep it silent. The others joined him, but the Shrieker began to retaliate, lunging at them with snapping jaws and swiping claws.

"Marjusina!" Lask shouted. "Read the bowl!"

While the others grappled with the creature, Marjusina scrambled over and squinted to see the writing around the edge of the bowl. It was dusty and worn, obscuring some of the symbols.

"Hurry up!" came Lask's impatient call as he ducked one of the Shrieker's kicking feet.

"Just a minute," huffed Marjusina. She blew a breath over the dustiest section, trying to make out the last few words, then nodded. "We have to drown it in the bowl!" she shouted.

"In that little thing?" yelped Forge.

The Shrieker let out another piercing cry, which was quickly silenced by Myranda's sword pommel cracking against its jaws.

"Drive it to the pedestal!" Lask told them.

They hacked and shoved at the beast, pushing towards the center of the room. Its tail whipped around, sweeping Forge's feet out from under him and kicking at Messalo, sending the griffin sprawling. Forge rolled back to his feet, stabbing at the monster, and it recoiled from him, finding Lask's boot heel in its chest. It was beaten back against the pedestal, and wasting no time, Lask and Forge grabbed it by the ears and forced its head under the water.

The creature flailed, struggling and sputtering, but Lask and Forge clung on. Messalo leapt onto its back, trying to still its throes. The Shrieker kicked and bucked, but they refused to let it go, keeping its muzzle shoved into the dark water. All of a sudden, it burst, dissolving into the water from whence it came, raining over their feet, and dropping Messalo to the floor with its sudden disappearance.

"Good heavens," said Marjusina, fluffing her hackles. "The book didn't say anything about *that*."

"Makes me wonder what else we might have to do," Lask remarked.

"I believe that's the next chamber," Marjusina said, crossing the room toward the set of stairs leading down, "It's a room of keys and a locked door. Nothing that wants to eat us, as far as I know."

They followed the passage onward and sure enough, they came to another chamber. It was even larger than the last, and it was lined floor to ceiling in thousands, perhaps millions of keys, in iron, copper, silver, gold and every metal in between. They hung ten or twenty deep from countless hooks, and were strewn across the floor several inches deep. On the other side was a tall wooden door.

"We have to find *one* key in all of this?" asked Forge.

"Apparently," muttered Marjusina, not having realized the sheer scope of the room. She crossed the chamber to inspect the door. "I don't know how Kaeron managed it."

"Could he have left the proper key nearby?" Lask inquired.

"The lock changes with each visitor, as I understand," the griffin replied. "The key could be anywhere." She squinted at the lock. "We're looking for one that's small, most likely black iron."

"There's thousands of iron keys," groused Messalo. "Is there nothing else to help narrow it down?"

Marjusina shook her head, at a loss.

"It did take Kaeron a day or so to find it, if memory serves," she said.

"We can't afford to waste a day looking for one key," Lask said. He looked at the door. "I wonder if the Gateway would know how to open it?" He closed his eyes, trying to find the Ancient with his mind. He could still feel Gonamadé, far away in the south and tried to figure out how to contact him.

Are you looking for me? came Gonamadé's voice suddenly.

Yes, Lask replied, *I'm glad I found you.*

All you have to do is say something, said the Ancient. *What do you want?*

We're in a room full of keys and only one fits the door. It could take days to find the right one and we don't have that long. Can you open it or tell us which key we need?

Let me see the door, said Gonamadé.

How?

Just open your eyes, silly.

Lask obeyed and approached the door, looking it over. It was a bizarre sensation, as if someone were standing behind him, looking over his shoulder.

Yes, I can open that, said the Ancient. *Put your hands on the door.*

Lask obeyed.

This is probably going to be a little painful, but I don't think it will kill you.

You don't THINK it will kill me? Lask demanded.

Gonamadé didn't answer. All of a sudden a jolt shot down Lask's arms and a white-hot pain exploded through his hands. It would have been instinctual to yank his hands back from the door, but Lask found he couldn't move. No part of him obeyed his mind, and he found himself trapped within his own body. Another jolt zapped through him into the door.

Gonamadé! Lask yelped.

Sorry, said the Ancient, *Just a little more.*

Another stinging, burning wave of magic pierced

through him, and Lask wondered if this was what it would feel like to be struck by lightning. It was as if every inch of his skin was on fire, black spots floating in his vision, then all of a sudden it stopped and there was a click in the door. Lask's motion returned and he immediately backed away from the door, entire body aching.

Sorry about that, said Gonamadé, sounding guilty. *It's much harder to conduct magic through you since I'm no longer within you.*

Thanks, Lask muttered, grudging, but grateful.

He felt the Ancient withdraw.

"Are you alright?" asked Myranda, concerned.

"I'll be fine," Lask said. "Come. Let's press on."

They passed through the doorway into a smaller chamber. When Messalo had slunk in behind them, the door shut, locking itself once more. There was no other door in the chamber. The room was empty, except for a single torch burning on the wall. As soon as they had all entered, it flared, sparks leaping from it, and suddenly there appeared a great wall of flame before them. The flames twisted and shaped themselves into a broad equine form. It tossed its head, blazing mane lapping around its face, and stamped its hooves, sending up sparks from the floor. It galloped in a circle around them, letting out a crackling whinny. They could feel its heat radiating over them and feared to think what would happen should it gallop any closer.

"Give me the name!" it roared.

"What name?" asked Marjusina.

"The name!" it demanded.

"Could we have a hint?" asked Forge.

It snorted a puff of sparks at him and stamped an impatient hoof.

"Give me the name of the one Mystery!" it said.

"The one mystery?" repeated Marjusina.

The horse cantered around them, drawing closer.

"Caledria," Lask said.

The horse stopped in its pacing to growl,

"What did you say, Somadar's blood? Speak a false name and I shall sear that pale skin from your bones!"

The others glanced at him, wary.

"Caledria," Lask said again, louder. "Mystery's name is Caledria."

The horse of fire tossed its head.

"Correct," it said.

The others let out the breath they'd been holding. The fire horse trotted over to the far wall, and blew a puff of flame out over the stone. An archway appeared in the wall, opening the way.

"Pass," it said, "And behold the Spring of Life."

Chapter Fourteen

Ariana was reading in the parlor and heard the knock on the door, though decided not to get up, since her mother's footsteps were already heading to answer it. She could hear the familiar voice of the Etherian scout, Verdin, who came often to deliver messages to her father. Ari got up and sauntered out, as Verdin was a particularly handsome young man, and Ari thought it would be a shame to miss a chance to satisfy her eyes. He smiled at her when she appeared around the corner.

"Would you like to stay and rest for a while?" Rhia asked him.

"That's quite alright, lady," he replied. "I shall take an easy pace back and probably stop in one of the villages for the night."

"Ah, Verdin," came Salazar's voice as he approached, "I'd hoped you'd come soon."

"You have letters for me, I assume, sir?"

"I do indeed." Salazar passed over the correspondence and Verdin tucked them away in his satchel.

"Anything urgent?" asked the messenger.

"No. No need to hurry."

Verdin gave a grateful nod and went back out to his horse. Rhia shut the door and passed the letters that had arrived over to Salazar. He took a cursory look through them and paused.

"One for Ari," he said, pulling it out of the stack. "Not anyone's writing I know."

Ari took it, eager, and retreated back to the parlor to tear into it.

Dearest Ariana, it read, *I have thought of you often since our meeting at the Denmahi festival last week. It was such a pleasure to at last speak to you. You are a truly captivating lady, and I wish very much to see you again. As I know that will not be possible for some time, I hope you will oblige me with a letter in return, so to satisfy this longing you have set within me. Best regards, Drake.*

"It had better not be from that solider," Salazar growled from out in the foyer.

Ari's grin betrayed her.

"You do realize he's older than *I* am?" said Salazar. "I won't stand for that."

Ari made an irritated noise. She and her father were exceptions when it came to Immortal aging. As both she and Salazar had been raised on Earth, they had aged at a mortal's rate, rather than the more gradual maturation of the Immortals. Had Drake been a mortal, he would have only been nineteen or twenty, a physical age that Ari found more than acceptable.

Rhia waited until Salazar had blustered away, then grinned at Ari to whisper,

"Write back. He seems like a nice man."

Ari grinned at her mother, but bit it back as Salazar trudged back into the room. For a moment, she thought he had overheard them and had returned to fuss some more, but instead he walked past them, as if unseeing, and sank into his chair before the fire. A letter fell from his hand and drifted to the floor like a leaf. Ari recognized her grandfather's tall pointy writing on the page.

"Adar?" she ventured.

He glanced back, as if just remembering his wife and daughter were there.

"The Mirror of Dùmsaro is free," he said.

Rhia exchanged a concerned glance with Ari.

"Have we been called back to Etheria?" asked Rhia.

"No, not yet." His voice was quiet, dazed.

"Then what—?"

"It has taken Scoarin."

Rhia's brow furrowed, and Ari, who had read more than her mother, put her head down, knowing well the implication.

"She has vanished to an unknown time and place on Earth," Salazar continued. "Adar says we may never see her again. He speaks of her as though she has died."

Rhia rose and went to put a hand on his shoulder. He reached up to hold her fingers.

"She was the first person I ever met in Etheria," he murmured. "Fildahorr was so angry." A faint smile brushed at his lips. "She took me away anyway, flew me to all sorts of places in one night. She was always so kind to me."

"And to me," Ari said, for it had been Scoarin to first tell her of her power as the Dreamweaver.

Salazar nodded, face awash in sadness. A sudden thought occurred to Ari.

"I could find her," she said.

"Not even the Ancients know where she is," Salazar replied.

"So?" Ari retorted. "I have called her in dreams many times. Why should I not be able to do it again?"

"She could be anywhere. Thousands of years in the past or future."

"I will find her." Ari spoke the words like a vow. "I will."

Chapter Fifteen

Ossifer and Morpheus followed the glow of Androla up ahead. They had soared into the mountains after the Spirit, far from any civilization. The light suddenly dropped into a ravine and the griffins tucked their wings to dive after her. The way was narrow, and Ossifer could feel the tips of his feathers catching on the sides of the canyon.

Androla's light stopped and she reformed on a ledge where there was an opening in the stone. The griffins landed beside her, squeezing in on the narrow ledge.

"It is a long way into the mountain and dark. I can lead you, but do not fall behind."

"We won't."

Androla's figure dissolved again into the shifting light and she drifted into the darkness. The griffins followed her into the mouth of the cavern. It was black as night inside; so dark, even the griffin's sharp eyes had a hard time seeing. It seemed to swallow Androla's light, and Ossifer and Morpheus walked close to her. The way was utterly silent, broken only by the soft padding of their feet and the rustling of their feathers. The passage narrowed so they had to walk single-file to get through as the path sloped down into the core of the mountain.

"How much farther?" whispered Ossifer, though he did not know why he kept his voice low.

"A fair distance yet."

Morpheus shuddered. Griffins were creatures of the open air and this still, coffin-like tunnel had them both on edge. After what felt like an eternity, they came to a set of wide stairs. Androla said there were many, but the ceiling was too low for the griffins to fly up. They began the climb, having to keep their heads low to avoid the sloped ceiling, unable to see just how far the stairs stretched on through the darkness. They seemed to go on for miles and after a while Ossifer and Morpheus were both panting.

"It is not far now," said Androla.

The two griffins pushed on, gasping as they finally reached the top, emerging into a vast chamber. It was illuminated by strange golden light, breaking the oppressive darkness that had followed them and stinging their eyes. In the center of the room was a dark tree, its branches thick and coiling, deep green leaves clothing its limbs. The tree shimmered with pulsing gold lights and as the griffins stepped in closer, they realized that each of the lights was a butterfly. They were enormous, having at least a foot wide wingspan.

"When you touch them," said Androla, "They will turn to gold. But be careful, for they are very poisonous. A bite will mean a slow death for you."

"We're just finding this out *now*?" Morpheus said to his father.

"Just be careful," said Ossifer. "Try to touch the wings, not the body."

Ossifer stalked in close to the tree, slowly extending a hand toward the closest butterfly. Sensing the intruders, the butterflies all flew up off the tree with surprising speed, flitting and fluttering out of reach. Ossifer opened his wings and chased after them, Morpheus joining him in the air. The butterflies evaded them, spinning and swooping, far too acrobatic and nimble for their size. The griffins rolled and wheeled in the air, batting at them, but they parted before their paws. Morpheus flew up above their mass and dropped into the middle of them, and there was a clang as one plummeted down to clatter to the ground, solid gold.

"Good work!" Ossifer squawked, landing to pick it up.

"Not quite," Morpheus groaned, landing beside him. He held out his hand, revealing two punctures in his finger. He winced. “It burns, like white fire.”

“Come,” Androla said, “I do not know of a cure for this, but perhaps your Ancients can help you. We must get you to them as quick as we can!”

Chapter Sixteen

Lask passed through the archway first and his companions followed. They emerged into a huge cavern, though it seemed to be a rocky meadow under a crystalline sky. Lask guessed that it must have been some sort of magical illusion, for they were still deep under the mountains and so could have no view of the sky. Rich grass covered the cavern floor, and flowers of all colors blossomed across the ground and along the walls from climbing vines. The air was cool and fragrant. It was a wild garden, a place that had been touched by the finger of God, the place where all life in their world had begun.

The cavern was dominated by the biggest tree any of them had ever seen. The oldest of its kind, the Eurydicen somehow remained graceful in its size. Its pale trunk was so thick, Lask thought that ten men could not have joined hands around it. Its branches spread out over the cavern in a canopy of lush green leaves edged in gold. It was laden with pale pink blossoms, fine petals drifting down like snow. From its labyrinthine roots came a rushing spring of crystalline water.

Lask approached the tree, feeling tiny beneath it, and reached out to place a long-fingered hand upon its trunk. He could feel the deep thrum of its life under his fingers and felt a deep sense of peace settle over him as he stood beside the waters.

"Drink," said Marjusina, settling down by the stream, "It's the best thing in the world for you."

They all knelt down in the velvety grass and Lask cupped his hands to dip them into the water. It rushed over his fingers like cold satin and he brought it to his lips, taking a cold, crisp drink that carried a satisfying sweetness, like nectar from a perfect flower. He imagined he could feel the water spreading through his veins, tingling along his skin. The lingering ache from Gonamadé's magic disappeared from his body. It was as if he breathed deeper, could feel the pulse of the world under his feet. All the colors seemed brighter; a new sense of hope and wonder blossomed in his heart.

He settled among the roots of the tree, feeling as though he could stay there forever. His companions did the same after they had drunk their fill and Forge had collected a bit of the water in a phial. They sat in silence together on the soft grass, resting in the cradling roots of the Eurydicen, no need for words.

There was a ripple in the water and Marjusina nudged Lask whispering,

"It's the river spirit."

Sure enough, the waters rippled and frothed, rising up to form a great serpentine head, like a dragon's, but one that seemed smooth and gentle. It blinked eyes of blue water at them.

"Welcome," it said, its voice gurgling but strangely musical, "I have waited for you Lask Somadar, and you also Myranda, Forge, Marjusina and Messalo."

"You know us," Lask said, already on his feet and approaching the water.

"I know you well," the water replied. "I have known you since before your conception. I know your fathers and your fathers' fathers. I am the Long Life, the very essence of Immortality. I am the Great One's gift to you. Long have I awaited your coming."

"How did you know we would come?" Lask asked.

"I know all there is to know about this world," the water replied. "I am no Ancient, nor Spirit, nor seer. I am simply eternity. You have felt my presence in your soul your entire life, and I have felt you. We are all one in the vast ocean of eternity." It turned, looking away downstream. "Come," it said. "I will show you the way out."

Its serpentine body slithered, moving with the current away downstream and Lask and the others followed it, walking along the bank, watching it with looks of amazement and awe. It led them through the cavern into a narrower, winding passage, until the stream fell away over a precipice, into the depths of the world. The water serpent bowed its head down to the rock and a rumble echoed off the stones.

An archway appeared in the cavern wall on the other side of the falls and a bridge of stone grew up out of the floor, arcing over to the opening, leading out into the mountains beyond.

"There," said the waters, "You will be safe. Before you go, I would like to help you. The road before you is great and difficult. I exist in all ages of this world and while I cannot interfere in the lives unfolding beyond these falls, I would answer you a single question. Ask of me whatever you will and I shall answer you."

Lask hesitated, wanting to know all sorts of things, but not knowing which would be best to ask. He glanced to his companions, who all waited, expectant. Unable to decide on a single question, Lask said to the waters,

"You know the road that we must walk. I ask that you prophesy for us. What must we know to travel that road?"

"A wise question," the waters replied.

Marjusina was fumbling with the satchel that Forge carried, scrambling for a piece of paper and ink to write as the waters began to speak,

> "Thy ally says, 'eye for an eye,' although
> the trade shall not be even. Leash thine ire
> or else the fire shall spread, and thus spreading
> consume the ones you once called Friend. Beware
> the rise of one once dead, beware the day on which
> he comes, but fear ye not the darkness
> that he shall lead forth in the night. For Time
> cannot erase mistakes, but swallow pride
> and heal them. Find the One Who Death Forgave
> and let him lead thee to the cursed one.
> Then stand before the gates of Hell and be
> thou not afraid. For though the bell of Death
> shall toll, it tolls but for the wicked."

"Thank you," Lask said, though he knew not what the waters meant.

"Go," said the waters, "And live. Fare thee well. We shall never meet again."

With that, the waters rippled, the head of the serpent flowing apart and falling away over the falls. Lask stepped out onto the bridge and crossed the chasm to the archway, he and his companions emerging on the mountainside. The archway closed behind them and the Spring of Life disappeared from view.

Chapter Seventeen

The sun was hot even in the early spring as Julius flew through the Barren Region. It was a vast, flat desert, the color of rust or dried blood. Craggy peaks surrounded it to the north and west, but once over them, the land leveled out into flat, empty nothingness. Julius and his small patrol of fairy soldiers flew high above the dusty ground where the air was cooler, until the dark shape of the Hydra fortress came into view. Julius told his men to land and stay put, flying on to the castle by himself.

The fortress was the largest structure in all Etheria. Black stone, it towered to immeasurable heights and sprawled in a wide berth across the landscape. Every door and window was enormous, so to accommodate the immense creatures that resided there. Julius tucked his wings to land, boots sending up small swirls of dust as they hit the ground. He approached the guards at the gate.

They were huge beasts, as large as dragons, but thicker-bodied, with big feet and tails like tree trunks. Five heads sprouted from each of their shoulders, and they all looked toward him as he approached.

"What do you want, fairy?" spat one. "Surely Aldebaran was clear enough to the last United messenger?"

"Then I suppose it's just as well I'm not here as one of the United," Julius replied, unafraid. "Cazour and I have corresponded these past months and I've come to pay him a visit. I have some news I'm sure he will be eager to hear."

One of the guards turned and lumbered inside.

"Yes, go," drawled Julius. "Fetch Aldebaran. No one can make a decision without him."

The remaining guard hissed at him with all five heads. Sure enough, it wasn't long until the deep blue hydra called Aldebaran, the second in command of the Hydras, appeared at the gate.

"King Cazour has been expecting you," said the hydra. "Come."

Julius followed the hydra inside, feeling dwarfed as he walked beside the creature.

"How is it he expects me?" asked the fairy. "I have not given him any indication I meant to come."

"His seer, Syringa, told him to expect the coming of a

blue-winged fairy. I assume that would be *you*."

Julius said nothing more, not having known the Hydras had a seer among them. He followed Aldebaran into the massive keep and down the entrance hall to the court of the Hydra King. It was a vast, long room, supported by three rows of thick columns on either side. Arched windows high above let in the light. At the other end of the room were steps leading up to a tier where another hydra stood. He was stony grey with iron claws and yellow eyes. His deep voice echoed through the vast hall,

"Julius. We meet at last."

"I consider it an honor, your majesty."

"Come," said Cazour, beckoning him up the stairs, "Speak with me."

Julius obeyed, deciding to open his wings and fly up rather than attempting to climb the massive stairs. The Hydra King settled down on an enormous cushion and motioned for the fairy to come sit beside him.

"I bring word—"

"Of the Mirror of Dùmsaro, I hope," rumbled the hydra.

"Yes," Julius said, trying to hide his surprise. "No doubt your seer told you."

"Indeed. I wish to possess it. It would bring me great power with which to rival the kingdom that challenges my dominion. Perhaps you can help me acquire it."

"That is what I wished to speak to you about," Julius replied. "The United are attempting to summon the Spirit Lothanvar, whose power created the Mirror, in order to destroy it. If you wait until they have summoned him, you could bring not only the Mirror but the most powerful of the Merrui under your control."

"I imagine there is something you want from me, else you would not be here," Cazour said, his other four heads coiling around one another, "Not when you could take the Mirror and this Spirit for yourself and slight me."

"We know each other too well," Julius answered with a crooked smile. "You are correct. Without some help from you, the Merrus cannot be summoned."

"What do you require of me?"

"An eye."

All of the hydra's heads turned to look at him.

"This is a steep price," he said. "And there is no guarantee we will be able to get the Mirror or the Spirit away from the United. What do you offer me in return?"

"My service," Julius replied.

"*You?*" said Cazour. "What good is one puny fairy to me? I need soldiers. My hydras do not number very many now. While I imagine we could damage the United and the kingdom they serve, their numbers would eventually win out, I wager."

"I command four thousand soldiers," Julius replied.

"And can you guarantee their loyalty?" asked the hydra. "For you swore your service to the United and yet you would betray them. What is to say you will not do the same to me?"

"I do not hate you as I hate their leader. I desire nothing more than to shame him and prove that he is not nearly as competent and inspiring as everyone believes him to be."

"You should be careful, fairy," teased the hydra, "For you smell strongly of jealousy." His heads grinned. "But jealousy is a powerful motivator."

"It is not jealousy. It is the rage of one who has been underestimated and taken for granted for too long," Julius growled.

"To betray the Somadar is an act of treason," remarked Cazour, "You and all of your kind shall be traitors."

"Then I suppose we will have one more thing in common."

The Hydra King let out a low, rumbling chuckle.

"I like you, Julius," he said. "I will send a few of my hydras to collect you from the United soon. I look forward to seeing your camp outside my castle." He lowered his central head down to the floor in front of the fairy, turning so to offer a sharp yellow eye. "Make it quick."

Chapter Eighteen

It was early afternoon two days later when Lask and his companions returned to the camp. They handed the water off to the Ancients, and when they did so, Gonamadé announced,

"We've learned how to collect the light of Autrial."

"Excellent. How?" Lask asked.

"It can only be harvested from the reflection of phoenix tears, which means you will be needing to make a journey to the Phoenixes' mountain."

"Me?" said Lask.

"Yes, of course. The phoenix Diem saved your life, so they obviously like you." Gonamadé grinned at him.

"Fine," Lask said, resigned. "We'll leave tomorrow."

He left the Ancients to inform the council of their success at the Spring and as he was walking back to his tent, he caught sight of a cloaked figure sitting by one of the fires, slender legs crossed, exposing porcelain ankles.

Lask considered ducking down one of the other rows to avoid her, but he had already been spotted. Mystery stood and sauntered over, cloak swishing with the sway of her hips. She came and patted a slender hand on his chest, lips smiling at him and saying,

"A simple thank you will do."

"Thank you," Lask replied, though a bit grudging.

"If you ever need to know something," she whispered, "All you have to do is ask."

"Ask?" Lask echoed, intrigued, despite himself.

Mystery smiled, trailing her fingers along the line of his collarbone and down his arm.

"I am not like Chai Karan or the Gateway," she said. "I can confide my secrets in whomever I want if they ask the right question. Though I might ask for a favor or two in return." She toyed with his fingers and gave him an enticing look from under her hood.

Lask pulled his hand away, saying,

"I'll keep that in mind."

Before he could return to his tent, Lask's eyes were drawn up to a movement in the distance. He caught sight of a fluttering pair of blue wings and went to meet Julius on the perimeter as the fairy and his patrol returned.

"Were you able to see the Hydra King?" Lask inquired.

Julius smirked and reached into his satchel, pulling

out a blood-soaked handkerchief, tossing it at Lask. Lask caught it on reflex, only to find himself holding an enormous, gory yellow eyeball, a few pieces of lint from the handkerchief clinging to its cornea. Lask resisted the urge to drop it and quickly kept his face from twisting into a look of total disgust to say,

"Thank you. Most successful, I see."

"Quite," the fairy replied, looking satisfied at Lask's revulsion.

"And the Hydra King was willing to do this once you explained the situation?"

"Most willing."

"That's very good news," Lask replied. "Fiora has been wanting to open negotiations with them for sometime. This may prove to be the cooperative gesture she's been waiting for."

"We should be sure to tell her of it."

Chapter Nineteen

For six nights, Ariana had searched in vain. She was not dismayed, for she knew she had not come close to exhausting her efforts. Instead, she found in her room a gold hair comb that Scoarin had given her on her last birthday. It had come from the dragon's hoard, and Ari suspected Scoarin had slept on it for years when she curled around her vast pile of treasure to rest. It was the only token she had from the dragon, and she decided it would have to do.

She placed the comb under her pillow and drifted off to sleep. She let herself sink deeper and deeper, calling the dragon's name out across the vast sea of dreams and sleepers. *Scoarin... Scoarin...* She called for hours, drifting across the world, across the centuries, calling and calling.

Then, there was a faint whisper.

"Ariana."

Ari seized onto it like a wolf on the kill and pulled

herself toward the source.

"Ariana!" The voice was louder.

"Scoarin!" She shouted. "I'm here!"

She felt a faint spark in the dream and drew it forward. The golden shape of the dragon materialized out of the fog and lay before her.

Scoarin looked tired and pale. There were stains on her face, and Ari knew she had been weeping.

"Ariana!" the dragon cried. "Is it you? Are you here?"

"I am," she answered. "I knew I could find you."

"Or at least, what is left of me to find," the dragon murmured and curled herself up, tucking her tail around herself.

"Where are you?" asked Ari. "*When* are you?"

"I do not know," Scoarin said, voice quiet, "Only that the world has moved far on from when last I was here. I used to the stars to make my way to what was Letiana and Kwynn. Indeed, I only knew the land by the coastline. The rest of it has changed so much. There are great metal cities and machines that spout black smoke. I followed the stars, followed the pull in my heart, and sought the Gate."

"Yes!" Ari said, "Surely it won't matter when you are now. If you can find it, you can still come home."

"Alas," the dragon cried. "There is no Gate."

The words hit Ari like a kick in the chest.

"I found the place where it should be, but it is there no more."

"Perhaps it was only moved—"

"No, child. It is gone. There were warauls there, but only a few. They were half wild; some could hardly remember the words of speech at all. The one called Azarak told me a terrible tale. I could not bear to repeat it to you."

Ari was silent, her heart aching for a tragedy she knew nothing of, not yet. She reached out to the dragon, resting a hand on her bowed head.

"How can I help you?" she asked.

"There were three others taken by the Mirror long ago."

As Scoarin spoke, a vision appeared in the dream and she saw thin man hunched over the Mirror, which was laid out on the stone floor of a cavern by the river. He was chanting horrible words, until a huge black shape appeared. Ari watched as the Merrus struck down the man who had summoned him, then reached to the Mirror and pressed a dark hand to its surface. The Mirror glowed with green light and a hideous face appeared. It spoke, but Ari could not hear its words. The Spirit left the cavern and the vision changed.

Lu`corian was there, her great-great-great grandsire. He roared back at the Merrus, his fabled sword cutting into the dark smoke with a flash of golden sparks. The Spirit was caught, but the Mirror escaped. Scoarin's voice came again.

"Ranseor, father of Vatron."

A tall gold dragon, with red edges on his scales, flailed in the clutches of green light.

"Adelina, sister of Falron."

A proud black dragon with blue frills screamed, pierced through the heart with the terrible green magic.

"Falsanthur, father of Navar."

An old blue dragon with a silver mane made no sound as the magic wrapped around him, only turned his head with mournful eyes toward an egg that was left behind.

"And now Scoarin, mother of Calliban."

Ari saw the scene unfold before her: the Mirror appeared in Scoarin's lair. She pushed Calliban back behind her as the magic cracked forward. She struggled but it was no use. The Ancients rushed in, with Lask close behind them, but they were too late and the Mirror was too strong. She cried out to Lask and then to her son, and then she was gone.

The visions faded and Ari stroked the dragon's head, wishing she could find the words to comfort her, but none came.

"You have found me," said Scoarin. "Perhaps you

could find the others. Perhaps we could meet at some time, so that we need not be so alone."

"If there are dragons left in the world," Ari said, "I will find them for you."

Chapter Twenty

It was late in the night when Lask awoke to the sound of shouting. Concerned, he shifted free of Myranda and pulled on his cloak and boots, going out to the perimeter to find Ossifer shouting,

"My son! Come, we must go to him!"

"What's happened?" Lask asked.

"Morpheus, he was bitten by the butterfly," exclaimed Ossifer, "We almost made it back, but he could not fly anymore. I could not carry him alone."

"Come on," Lask said, motioning for the nearest soldiers.

They followed the griffin away from the camp, two of the soldiers carrying torches to light the way through the darkness. It was not quite a mile from the camp that they spotted a strange light. As they approached, Lask realized the light was in the shape of a woman.

"She is a Terwinus," Ossifer explained, "She's been

helping us. I'll explain later."

Morpheus lay in a heap where he had fallen out of the sky. The griffin's body shook with tremors and chills, his breath coming in rattling wheezes. Ossifer braced himself against his son and Lask and the soldiers filed in around him, hefting the shaking griffin up between them. They made their way back toward the camp, the Spirit drifting along behind them. When they reached the camp, Ossifer said,

"Call for the Ancients. Androla says they are the only ones who might be able to help him."

"Go," Lask told one of the soldiers, and the man took off running.

They lay Morpheus out in the healers' tent and the healer on duty there brought a few blankets to drape over the shivering griffin. Not a moment later, Socadan barged into the tent, the Gateway and Time in tow.

"Get out of the way!" the old wizard exclaimed, shoving the soldiers out of his path. "Where'd it bite him?"

"His hand," said Ossifer, gesturing.

"Did you get the fangs out?"

"The fangs?"

"Damn it all, you feathered fool!" Socadan knelt down in front of Morpheus, finding the wound, and promptly squashed it with his fingers.

Morpheus squawked and flailed, the sudden pain

lending him strength.

"Hold still, you great brute!" groused the wizard, and squeezed again. Two small slivers resembling splinters were pushed up out of the bite. Socadan plucked them off and set them on one of the healer's trays nearby. He held a hand to the griffin's head, feeling his fever. "How long ago was he bitten?"

"Day before yesterday," Ossifer replied.

Socadan sighed and shook his head.

"What?" asked Ossifer.

"The longer the fangs stay in, the faster the poison can spread. It's been too long."

"What are you saying?"

"There's nothing we can do."

"Surely the Ancients can do something," said Lask, "You have great healing magic."

"It has been too long," Chai Karan repeated. "Even if we could draw all the poison out of him, he would likely still die. Perhaps had he been brought to us sooner—"

"You can stop Time, but you can't cure a poison?" Lask demanded.

"If we had more time to prepare an antidote, we probably could, but he'll be dead in a matter of—"

"The water," Lask said suddenly. "The water from the Spring of Life."

"We can't use that—"

"It would probably only take a few drops," said the Gateway.

"And every drop we do not use on the Merrus is less magic to bind him with," Chai Karan shot back. "He was difficult enough to bind before, surely you remember that. And now with the Mirror to help him, *any* weakness in the magic could—"

"But he's dying," said Gonamadé.

"One griffin is not worth—"

"*Yes, he is,*" Lask snarled. "The water. *Now.*"

"If we waste *any* of that, it will—"

Gonamadé silenced Chai Karan by shoving him out of the way. The Gateway reached into his robe to produce the phial of Spring water. He knelt down by Morpheus's head, uncorking the phial and holding the griffin's head to allow a few drops to fall into his beak. The effect was almost immediate. Morpheus's tremors eased and his breathing fell back into a normal rhythm. Gonamadé nodded and put the stopper back in the phial, replacing it in his robe. He stood up, Chai Karan glowering at him.

"He should be all better by morning," said the Gateway.

"Thank you," Ossifer replied. He gave a grateful nod to Lask.

Chai Karan just turned around and walked out.

Chapter Twenty-One

Lask awoke early the next morning to prepare for the journey to the Phoenixes' mountain. As Ossifer was still looking after Morpheus, Lask asked Marjusina if she'd been willing to fly them into the Arayan Mountains. The silver griffin was eager to go. Lask left orders with Forge to pass on to the council, then he and Myranda set out with Marjusina.

It was a pleasant day for a flight, clear and warm. The trees of the Carthonian rippled below them like a sea in the wind, the edges of their leaves still trimmed in gold from the departing winter. Lask noticed Marjusina seemed to be making an effort to keep her flight smooth, for which Lask was grateful. They landed as the sun was setting, deep in the heart of the Carthonian, far from any civilization, but Lask knew the wilderness well and led them to a place where they could shelter for the night.

An enormous oak grew on a knoll by the river, its

thick roots twining around the rocks, creating a sheltered hollow large enough for the two humans and the griffin to rest in comfortably. Lask gathered some wood for a fire, and while he did so, Marjusina caught them a few fish from the river and Myranda gathered some wild keppàs.

When morning came, they set out once more at first light. Marjusina caught a swift wind to the west, and it was noontide when they reached the Arayan Mountains. Lask directed Marjusina from the map he had brought, guiding her flight to the southwest to an isolated peak. The griffin circled it, until she spied an opening in the mountainside. When she landed, Lask and Myranda slid from her back, going to inspect it.

It was a stone archway leading into a dark passage. It was carved with intricate designs and sweeping text that neither of them could read.

"Domiel Phénicae," translated Marjusina, "Home of the Phoenixes."

Lask lit the torch they had brought and went in first. The way was dusty and winding, leading them into the center of the mountain to a great spiral stairway. They followed it up and up. The torchlight flickered on the walls, revealing innumerable carvings, showing all manner of creatures, depicting moments from both history and legend. The carvings were too smooth and flawless to have been made by ordinary hands and chisels. They could only be the work of magic.

The stairway led them to a chamber at the top of the mountain. There was a hole in the ceiling, allowing light to shine into a shallow basin that sat on a pedestal at the center of the hall. Ancient, worn columns surrounded the chamber and flowering vines climbed among them. There were rock outcroppings along the walls and graceful stalactites ornamenting the ceiling, extending pale fingers toward the rounded stalagmites on the floor.

Perched on the outcroppings and stalagmites were seven birds. They were large, the size of swans or perhaps a bit larger, and were all brilliant crimson, with gold tips on their feathers. Large crests of plumes adorned their heads and long, elegant tails trailed behind them. One gave a warbling whistle and flapped over, landing on Lask's outstretched arm. Lask knew the bird and said,

"Hello again, Diem."

The phoenix nodded and flitted over to sit on the nearest stalagmite, taking his heavy weight off Lask's arm. Another phoenix flew over, landing nearby, turning his proud head to inspect the newcomer with a sharp golden eye. He was the largest of them, with the longest tail and proudest crest on his head.

"Adverett," Lask said with a respectful nod, recognizing the phoenix as the oldest of them.

The phoenix gave a satisfied squawk. The rest of his fellows all flew over, landing around the trio of visitors and together they spoke in an echoing, layered voice neither male nor female,

"Welcome, travelers. We foresaw your approach so laid no magic to hinder you."

"We are grateful for that," Lask replied.

"Tell us what you seek from us, Somadar," they chorused.

"We must gather the light of Autrial, so that we may summon Lothanvar to destroy him and the Mirror."

"A worthy task," came the echoing reply. "The light shall be yours to have, but you must wait until the star rises and capture its light from the basin. We shall prepare it for you. You are welcome to rest here today and for the night."

"Thank you."

The Phoenixes nodded and one by one, they flew over to land on the pedestal, bowing their heads to weep pearly tears into the basin. They took turns doing so all afternoon, while Lask, Myranda and Marjusina settled down to wait. They were quiet, though they knew not why. There was no need to speak, and there was a hallowed hush in the Phoenixes' hall that they were loath to disturb.

There was a sacredness about the birds. They were mysterious creatures and little was written of them. They were Created after the Ancients and the First, but just before the rest of the world's creatures were made. They were a single mind, inhabiting seven forms, and possessed a great power of prophecy. It was believed they knew the future as well as Time himself, but they would share this knowledge with no one. They only emerged from the mountain at times of great need, and never had anyone seen all seven out at once. Indeed, to behold them together was a wondrous sight, and though they had hours to wait, not one of the onlookers grew tired of watching them.

Chapter Twenty-Two

Sutonius entered Julius's tent, carrying a sizeable bundle of papers.

"More letters from Finistrì," he said.

"They never end, do they?" muttered Julius from his place at the table. "Set them over there." He motioned to the other smaller table in the corner.

Sutonius obeyed, setting the letters down, but as he did so, his eyes were drawn to several of the other papers there. Curious, he noticed one was a map of the Barren Region, another was an order Julius had written for supplies; far more water than they normally needed, extra rations, shade cloths.

"What is this?" asked Sutonius.

"Don't concern yourself," Julius growled.

"If I didn't know better, I'd say you were planning on making a trek into the Hydras' territory." Sutonius looked back at him, and read the expression on his friend's face.

"*Are* you?"

"I said don't concern yourself."

"Does Lask know of this? The council?"

"They don't need to, and you had better not go running to them."

"Surely you are not serious!" Sutonius exclaimed, his sharp mind having reached the conclusion Julius wanted to keep hidden from him. "The Hydras are vicious and will do anything to keep their dominion."

"And are the United so different?" asked Julius.

"I don't know how you could possibly compare the two, let alone consider switching sides—"

Julius's wings snapped open and he lunged at his friend in an instant. Sutonius was tackled over in a tangle of limbs and wings. Julius pinned him there and Sutonius was stunned to find his friend's knife at his throat.

"Julius," he breathed. "What is happening to you?"

"If you should breathe a word of this to *anyone*—"

"Surely the rest of our kind will not stand for this—"

"I've already been working on that. Most of our soldiers already know and are making the necessary preparations."

"And you haven't told *me* about this, your second in command?"

"I knew you'd need a little more persuading," Julius hissed, pressing the knife in a little tighter for emphasis.

"Your senses always were clouded with so-called morality."

"I cannot let you do this," said Sutonius. "You cannot betray them—"

"If you should speak a word of this to the United, I will make you wish you were dead," growled Julius. "You have a cousin in Finistrì, don't you? He has two young daughters, doesn't he?"

"This has nothing to do with them," Sutonius snarled back.

"And that other cousin of yours, that vagabond, Montevale, who you love like a brother, who prefers the ocean and the company of humans to his own kind. I'm sure I could probably work a sentence of treason out for that somehow—"

"Have you lost your mind?"

Julius's knifepoint drew a small bead of blood out of the skin at Sutonius's vulnerable throat.

"Do you really want to find out?" he hissed.

Sutonius said nothing more, glaring up at him, hardly knowing the fairy who held him down. Julius released him and went back to the table, leaving Sutonius to get to his feet and shuffle out.

Chapter Twenty-Three

Fiora had set out that morning with an escort of ten soldiers. The Elinsara was making her way south toward the Barren Region, taking a brisk pace over the meadows toward the Plains. The news of the Hydra King's cooperation with the United had been a most welcome turn and brought her a fair amount of hope. The Hydras had been a restless, volatile race for millennia, ever since their first King, Kratorin, had died and his ruthless son Adalar had inherited the throne. Cazour, a descendent of Adalar, had proven to be even more vicious than his forebears and the Ambassador had begun to fear their relations could only end in war.

As she traveled, Fiora glanced skyward and noticed a trio of fairies flying high above them, speeded by the wind, disappearing to the south in the same direction of the Ambassador. Fiora was curious, but then decided they must be simple travelers or soldiers on another errand for the United.

Chapter Twenty-Four

Once the sun had set, Lask was able to see the heavens through the opening in the cavern ceiling. The Phoenixes were watching the sky too, waiting, ever patient, for the bright star Autrial to come into view. When at last it was positioned directly above them, they spoke once more,

"The time is right. Come forth and gather its light from the basin."

Lask rose and approached the pedestal, producing the phial the Gateway had given him to collect the light in. The shallow basin had been filled with the Phoenix's opalescent tears, and they seemed to shift and gleam with a light of their own. They reflected the sky and Lask saw the reflection of Autrial gleaming at the very center. Unsure of how it would work, he dipped the phial into the tears and the reflection of the star trickled into the phial. When he withdrew it, the reflection did not disappear, but rather, the tears continued to gleam with the starlight.

He placed the stopper back into the phial, then turned to bow to the Phoenixes, saying,

"Thank you."

Chapter Twenty-Five

Lask and Myranda returned to the United's camp on the back of Marjusina two days later. Socadan was waiting for them and the old wizard came stomping up when they landed saying,

"About time! What were you doing, you pasty prat? Taking a holiday?"

Lask was about to make an icy retort when Gonamadé came barging up, shoving Socadan out of the way to ask with an eager grin,

"Did you get it?"

Lask produced the phial, still glowing with starlight, and handed it over.

"Ah, excellent!" exclaimed the Gateway. "This is everything then. I think we can summon Lothanvar tonight, if that's alright by you."

"The sooner the better, I suppose," Lask replied.

Lask and Myranda went away in the direction of

their tent, and Gonamadé watched them go with a fond smile. Socadan was still muttering, but the Gateway ignored him, turning to go his own way through the camp. As he walked, he caught sight of Julius stalking through the rows of tents. At the sight of him, the Gateway stopped short, breath catching as the ancient prophecies came rushing back to the surface of his mind. In that moment, the Ancient remembered everything the fairy was going to do and the catastrophic horror that would stem from it.

Gonamadé turned away, unable to look at the fairy. He took off in another direction, mind reeling, torn. He knew the Ancients were meant to stay silent about their knowledge of the future, but he felt sick at the thought of what would happen if he did. He knew the pain that would befall the United, and the unfathomable pain and guilt that would later envelop Lask, and the Gateway did not know if he could bear the weight of it.

He was pacing back and forth around one of the fires, anxious tail twitching behind him, hands working over one another when Chai Karan came and settled down nearby to watch him, seeming almost amused at his nervousness.

"So restless, Gateway," Time remarked.

"We could stop this," said Gonamadé, pointing in the direction of the Fairies' section of the camp. "We could stop all of it. Just warn them. Julius could be imprisoned, no one would have to be hurt, Lask would never go to Finistrì and—"

"We cannot interfere," growled Chai Karan. "We were given strict instructions, bound to silence—"

"Maybe *you* were, but I don't remember Him ever saying—"

"It is not our place."

"We are a part of this world as much as they are!" the Gateway exclaimed. "We can keep them from hurting each other. We could save them—"

"It is not up to us whether they should be saved. Even I cannot know all the workings of the Plan. Certain things are meant to happen. We must hold our silence and let them, else we could disrupt everything the One intends for the future."

"But He is loving and benevolent. Surely He wouldn't—"

"It is not our place to presume what He intends."

"If He didn't want us to help them, he wouldn't have given us our own minds, judgments, souls—"

"Souls?" Chai Karan echoed. "Surely, Gateway, you do not believe that. We are *functions*, worldly rhythms and powers. We have no more soul than the tides!"

"But the tide cannot think or feel," said the Gateway. "How can I feel so terrible if I have no soul to be hurting?"

"It's your own silly delusions that are hurting," Chai Karan scoffed. "We're here to be placeholders to our functions and participate in history as we are instructed. We're not here to write history as we would have it—"

"Why not? *They* do!" protested the Gateway, gesturing at all the camp and creatures around him. "They can choose the paths of their lives—"

"Not all of them. You ought to know that; your beloved Uniter is a prime example."

"He's had plenty of say in his life," Gonamadé replied. "He's not just some puppet of fate and Time, as *you* would like to conveniently believe. He's already changed so much—"

"In accordance with the Prophecy."

"*Everything's* not prophesied."

"But they don't know that," growled Chai Karan. "They can choose their own paths because they do not know where those paths will lead. If you know the future, you are already changing it just by acting with that knowledge. Don't you see? If we do *anything* not specified by the One, then we risk *everything*."

Gonamadé put his head down with a sigh.

"That's another reason you took hosts, you know," Chai Karan remarked. "You didn't trust yourself. You knew if you weren't constrained you might go meddling—"

"You, of all of us, have no room to speak of *meddling,*" growled Gonamadé.

He gave his fellow Ancient a venomous look and stalked away. Chai Karan looked after him with nothing more than an amused smile.

Chapter Twenty-Six

It was sunset when Lask followed Gonamadé to Scoarin's cave where the Ancients were preparing to summon Lothanvar. They walked in silence and Lask could feel the gnawing worry seeping over into his mind from Gonamadé's. It was a bizarre sensation and Lask wondered if he would ever get used to it.

"Are you alright?" he asked of the Ancient.

"Fine," Gonamadé muttered.

Lask felt the Ancient withdraw a bit in his mind, as if trying to conceal his anxiety, which just made Lask all the more concerned.

When they arrived at Scoarin's (now Calliban's) cave, Socadan was already there, preparing the spell. He had a cauldron boiling over a small fire and was positioning the three diamonds Vatron had given him around the edge of it. Mystery was already there, having been standing guard over the Mirror all day, and Chai Karan had joined her.

Maléchian appeared in the Mirror's surface, watching them in silence, gaunt face unreadable.

"Good, we're all here," said Socadan.

Gonamadé passed the phials of Spring water and starlight to the wizard then went to stand beside the other two Ancients.

"Be ready," Socadan said to them, unusually quiet.

The wizard uncorked one of the phials and let the Spring water pour into the cauldron as he said,

"Esiel mesér esiò, feree advén esem cò el morthanén." He produced the sea serpent scale and dropped it in with a small splash. "Gairthén de nathairmari, actho nathòan en sapethòan, vaylie Merruén ad velo locùriòn." Socadan unwrapped the withering eyeball and let it plop into the cauldron. "Oculu vesdaré de Derilis Terraen, vidére ìad nunbraelòan en vidéle mesér praeathòn." He poured in the mermaid blood. 'Sathùniel de estellamari, adilergoe, actho sapethòan, rathairòn." He let the golden butterfly fall, splashing, into the cauldron. "Volarie, sapairnén unu, en athénie cùn Anionén nunbraelòn." [3]

[3] "Life of our life, bring forth the one who is dead. Scale of the sea serpent, by the treachery and guile of your kind, draw the Merrus to this place. Eye of the king of the Barren Land, see into the darkness and spot our quarry. Blood of the seamaid, bind the wicked by your cunning. Fly, elusive one, and return with the Spirit of darkness."

The wizard beckoned Mystery over. She approached and bent over the cauldron, letting the vapors wash over her face, and her reflection seemed to ripple in the water.

"Vesiaj de Arcael," said the wizard, "Érfore per arcanòan en feree advén unén sié petén."[4]

He motioned to Chai Karan. The drokamerdor bowed his head and hissed a breath into the cauldron.

"Spiranen de Témticiel," Socadan said, "Pertie per elopathòan ad morthané uné olivìòn fabunòn. Feree advén vé elapérbòn."[5]

The wizard uncorked the phial of starlight and poured it in. The light spilled out of the phial like gleaming quicksilver.

"Lùcùlén de Autrial, lùstriel de Lumiel, lùcrie ìad nunbraelòn en adilergoe aundién de nunbraelòn sìrm lùmiòan."[6]

Lask stood by, feeling the magic gather in the air, a crackling energy like the moment before lightning. Socadan raised his hands and produced one sharp clap,

---

[4] "Image of the Unknown, pierce through the mysterious to bring forth the one we seek."

[5] "Breath of Time, reach through the ages to the forgotten tale of the one dead. Bring it forth for the telling."

[6] "Brilliance of Autrial, spark of the Light, shine into the darkness and bind the creature of shadow with your light."

declaring,

"Actho brùnauno, sié envocantiel advén Lothanvarén Dùmsarén exo ordìnauno Merruni. Audintele mesérm, Anion, en ecthoaene velo vondellòn!" [7]

There was a blinding flash of red light, and Lask had to shield his eyes against it. He could hear Maléchian laughing, a high eerie cackle, and there was a rumble that shook the cavern floor. Before it subsided, there came a new sound, a grating roar that echoed off the stone and through the trees beyond.

"NOW!" came Chai Karan's shout.

Lask looked back to see a writhing black mist twisting in the center of the cavern. It materialized into a black shape, the torso of a huge man, though where there should have been hips and legs there swirled only dark smoke. Its skin was black, stretched taut over thick, bulging muscle. Black glinting eyes darted around the cavern.

The Ancients did not waste a moment. They released their magic in unison, gold cords of light lashing out, twining around the Merrus, catching his wrists and arms and around his neck. Socadan aided them, using his own magic to anchor the cords to the cavern floor, each with a resounding crack, binding the creature fast. The Spirit roared once more and boomed,

---

[7] "By these powers, we summon forth Lothanvar the Dùmsaro from the ranks of the Merrui. Hear us, Spirit, and answer this call!"

"Who summons Lothanvar?"

"That would be me," Socadan replied, "On behalf of the United Races of Etheria."

"Little wizard," hummed the Merrus. "I remember you, though how you have withered since our last meeting."

"Yes, well, you're not looking any better either."

Lothanvar ignored him, turning his head to catch sight of the Mirror.

"Maléchian!" he exclaimed, "What have they—?"

A bolt of golden light zapped out of the Gateway's finger, snapping faster around the Merrus's mouth before he could say any more.

"Can't have you two conspiring with each other," said Gonamadé.

Lothanvar glowered at the Ancient with hardened eyes.

"What now?" asked Lask.

The Spirit's eyes snapped over to him, but Lask ignored the glare.

"Chai Karan has to grapple with his mind to find the memory necessary to condemn him," said the Gateway. "Once he has it, he can take us back to collect it."

Lask didn't entirely understand, but trusted the Ancients to do what was needed.

"It will take time," Chai Karan said, "For he is very

strong."

"I have faith in you," replied Gonamadé, "You can wear down even the most dauntless of spirits."

Chai Karan gave the Gateway a look, but Gonamadé pretended not to notice.

Chapter Twenty-Seven

Lask got little sleep that night. Since Lothanvar had been summoned, a dark power seemed to vibrate in the air, keeping him constantly on edge. To make matters worse, he could still feel the Gateway fretting, the Ancient's mind turning and twisting over thoughts too fast and erratically for Lask to even try to eavesdrop.

He ended up lying awake all night, listening to Myranda's breathing on his shoulder, running his hand along her back, softly so not to wake her. He could not pinpoint the exact nature of his distress; he was only aware of something being terribly *wrong*. When morning came, he rose and rode to the dragon's cave.

Chai Karan was still at work, sitting before the Merrus, head bowed and eyes closed. Lothanvar, too, had his eyes closed, face set in a snarl. Socadan was keeping watch while the Mirror looked on in silence.

"He's still at it," the wizard reported. "The Merrus is stronger than he thought. He's not come out of his meditation to say, but I'm starting to guess perhaps the Mirror is lending Lothanvar strength. Being created from him, they must share some kind of connection."

"Can we move it elsewhere so that it cannot interfere?" asked Lask.

"Too late for that I'm afraid," Socadan answered. "To move either of them we'd have to temporarily ease the magic, and you know they'd bolt at the first chance they got. We have to keep them here until we're ready to deal with them. We thought we'd keep them together so to not spread our magic and concentration too thin, but in hindsight, perhaps we should have kept them separated."

This news did little to ease Lask's growing worry. When afternoon came, the council gathered.

"What progrezz wizh ze Zpirit?" asked Asmodeus.

"None yet," Lask told them. "Chai Karan is still working to find the memory we need to condemn him."

"I don't like this taking so long," said Vatron. "Every moment the Mirror is there is another moment it can use to escape."

"I don't like it any more than you do," Lask replied, "And I hope the Ancients can find what they need swiftly. I fear there is little any of us can do at this point."

"Which just makes it all the worse," groused Polian.

"What's the hurry?" asked Julius, almost teasing. "It's bound for the time being. Surely you don't doubt the Ancient's magic, Somadar?"

Sutonius cast a venomous look at his friend from the corner of his eye, a look that startled Lask, who noticed it. He said nothing, instead replying to Julius,

"I have faith in the Ancients' ability, but I do not trust our enemy."

Chapter Twenty-Eight

When the council disbanded, Lask was going to ask for a word with Sutonius, but the fairy disappeared before Lask could pull him aside. Julius went the opposite direction and Lask was suspicious, as the two were usually as close as brothers. He wandered the camp for a while, until he caught a glimpse of orange wings and went after them.

Sutonius slipped away again, but Lask pursued him, following the fairy at a distance through the camp, beginning to realize Sutonius was deliberately avoiding him. Lask ducked around the healer's tent and stepped across the fairy's path as he came around.

"Good evening, Sutonius," he said.

The fairy looked pale and tired, and he looked up at Lask as if he had suddenly encountered a bear in the woods.

"Good evening, commander," he replied. "Is there

something I can do for you?"

"I couldn't help but notice you and Julius seem to be at odds today. Is everything alright?"

Sutonius turned his eyes away toward the ground and Lask was struck at just how distraught the fairy looked. Sutonius looked back up to him with lost eyes and looked about to speak, but his lips closed again. The fairy glanced back to his shoes then caught sight of Julius in the distance behind Lask.

Julius gave him a pointed look and drew his knife, pointing it away toward the east where Sutonius knew Finistrì lay. The fairy glanced back to Lask, wanting more than anything to tell him. Lask stood there before him, expectant, concerned, every inch the noble lord the fairy wanted to serve, but he could not ignore the malevolent eyes that bored into him from a distance and could not stop his mind from imagining Julius's knife slitting the tender freckled skin of his cousin's two young daughters, who he loved like his own. For all the storm of rage and shame that stirred inside him, Sutonius could not find the courage in his heart to change it. Disgusted with his own weakness, he just shook his head and muttered,

"We're fine."

With that, he slipped away before Lask could question him further. Lask looked after him, troubled and wary, and glanced behind him, wondering what had kept the fairy from speaking, but by then, Julius was gone.

Lask made his way back through the camp, seeking out the Gateway, and again, he could not help but feel he was being avoided. Gonamadé was normally easy to find, but he was proving elusive. Lask didn't let him escape, following the pull of their mental connection until he finally cornered the Ancient in the center of camp.

"What's happening?" Lask demanded. "Something is not right and no one will tell me what it is. I know you know—"

"Don't ask me," begged Gonamadé, putting his head in his hands. "I cannot bear to cause you pain, but I cannot interfere. Please do not ask me." He hid himself behind a wing and slunk away and Lask looked after him with a growing feeling of dread, wondering what could quell the happy, hopeful spark that always flared in the Gateway.

"Ask..." Lask echoed to himself. An idea suddenly ignited in his mind and he took off at a jog through the camp, seeking a cloaked figure. He began to think she was avoiding him too, when he suddenly spotted her standing on the northwest perimeter, looking away toward the trees.

"Mystery!" he called.

She turned to him, and her lips did not smile at him from under her hood.

"It is too late," she said, voice laden with sorrow.

"For what?" Lask demanded. "What's happening? Tell me, *please*. I know something is wrong, but no one will tell me what it is."

Mystery stepped forward to him, reaching up to slip her hand under his hair to rest at the nape of his neck. Lask was wary as she pulled his head down to her, and she folded her other hand across his eyes, tilting her head up to sigh a warm breath over his ear.

A light suddenly flashed behind his eyes and Lask saw images unfold in his mind:

Julius sitting and talking with the Hydra King.

A knife.

Fairies, the entire army of fairies, flying into the darkening sky, away from the United's camp.

The rust-hued expanse of the Barren Region.

Sutonius bound, his wings in tatters.

Fairies filing into ranks among the Hydras.

Fire. Screaming.

"No," Lask breathed.

"It is too late," Mystery whispered in his ear.

A shout rang in the distance. Mystery released him and Lask was off running in an instant, following the source of the noise through the camp to the southern perimeter.

"What is it?" he called as he approached.

"There, sir," said one of the guards.

Lask looked out across the field as the sun was going down and saw the dark shapes of three hydras, galloping full speed straight for them.

"To arms!" Lask roared.

The hydras came plowing into the camp, heads snapping and roaring, feet crushing anything in their path. Lask had his sword drawn in an instant, ducking out of the way of one of the charging hydras, swinging back to hack at its leg as it passed. The hydra roared, but hardly stumbled.

"Get the dragons!" Lask called to his soldiers. "And bring me Julius! NOW!"

Several of the dragons were already running to the perimeter, drawn by the commotion. Calliban was among them and the young dragon flung himself at the nearest hydra, claws lodging into its back. The hydra flailed and rolled onto the ground, crushing several soldiers beneath it. Lask took a spear from a wounded soldier nearby and hurled it. It found its mark in one of the beast's roaring mouths, piercing into the throat of the dominant head. The creature thrashed and flailed, choking as it died.

Lask looked over his shoulder then and saw the image of Mystery's vision manifest before his eyes. From back in the camp, the Fairies were taking flight, rising into the darkening sky, flying up over the chaos and away to the south, not looking down at the struggle and plight of the ones they once called allies.

There was a sickening snap as one of the dragons snapped three of the hydra's necks with one sharp kick and the beast rolled, thrashing in its death throes. As Calliban sank his teeth into the central throat of the remaining one, Lask looked skyward to the departing hoard, picking out a familiar pair of blue wings in the dying light.

"JULIUS!"

The fairy banked and turned back for a moment, wings fluttering to keep him hovered overhead.

"How dare you?" Lask snarled up at him.

"You will curse my audacity, yet have nothing to blame but your own," the fairy replied. "Vortearigan was right about you, about all of you. The power of this kingdom is anything but fair—"

"Only because *you* cannot have it!" Lask shot back.

"*That* is exactly what I mean," Julius spat, pointing an accusing finger down at him. "It is that arrogance that has bought you a war."

"Vow war on this kingdom and I shall crush you!" Lask roared. "I shall salt the ground with the ashes of your kind!"

Julius drew back his arm and flung his knife down, but Lask sidestepped it, snatching it up out of the ground where the blade buried itself, brandishing it up at the fairy and swearing,

"This knife shall be the death of you."

Julius spat down at his feet, then turned, flying with the rest of his kind away into the darkness. Lask glowered after them, blazing, then looked back down to his soldiers and the dragons who were standing over the dead hydras.

"Gather the wounded and the dead," he told them. "Drag the hydras into the forest and leave them."

"But sir—" started one of the dragons.

The wrathful fires of Lask's gaze silenced the dragon without a word. He left his soldiers to clean up the mess, and swept off into the camp, calling for Forge. His friend was already running toward him, drawn by the chaos.

"What is it?" he demanded, "What—?"

"Julius and the Fairies are gone," Lask growled, "Gone to the Hydras. Find Calliban and go after Fiora with all speed. She's heading into enemy territory. We must catch her before they do."

Forge nodded and took off toward the perimeter to find Calliban. Lask continued into the camp, finding the Gateway sitting beside a fire with his head in his hands.

"You knew," Lask snarled at him. "You knew and you did *nothing*."

Gonamadé covered his face with his hands and Lask could feel the turbulent emotions stirring in him— guilt, shame, sorrow— but Lask did not care.

"*Look at me,*" he snapped. "Speak!"

Gonamadé raised his head, face tearstained.

"I can't," the Ancient whispered.

"Can't?" Lask echoed. "Or won't? You and the other Ancients knew we were going to be attacked and betrayed. You could have stopped all of this. You could have saved the lives of my soldiers who died tonight. You could have—"

"We can't interfere. Chai Karan—"

"I don't give a damn what Chai Karan says. You do not answer to him. How can you call yourself my friend when you stand by and let this happen?"

Gonamadé looked up at him, eyes still full of tears, then stood up, stepping forward to him to place a hand on his shoulder. Lask would have shifted free of him, but Gonamadé moved on before he could, walking back through the camp toward the wreckage and blood. The Ancient approached the scene where the wounded were being gathered and a voice said,

"Don't you dare."

Gonamadé looked to see Chai Karan standing there, watching him with sharp, demanding eyes.

"Don't you have Merrus to interrogate?" Gonamadé snapped.

"I know what you're doing—"

"Then go on! Try to stop me!"

"If you interfere you could throw off the entire Plan—"

"And who are you to know what the Plan is anyway?" demanded Gonamadé. "You may be the oldest among us, but you are *not* my lord."

"You will be judged—"

"Then let me be judged!" roared the Gateway. "Compassion is never a sin, not even for us! We were given free will and I shall use it. Do not presume to tell me my fate when you don't even know your own! Cower behind your laws and presumptions if you will, but I will not be a servant to them."

With that he flung open his arms as if to embrace the entire scene and from him burst the golden light of magic, sweeping out to the sound of Chai Karan's outraged roar. Sparks of magic flitted and flared over the wounded, healing even the deepest of wounds in a single burst. While he could not save the dead, the Gateway ensured no more would die, washing his magic over anyone who needed it. When he was finished, he dropped his arms, shoulders slumping, exhausted.

Chai Karan just looked at him, shaking his head, disgusted and disappointed, then turned away without saying a word. Lask went forward to put a hand on Gonamadé, but the Ancient trudged past him before he could speak a word of thanks.

"I must answer for what I have done," murmured the Gateway, voice so weary, the sound of it doused the rage that had been stirring in Lask, draining the wrath right out of him.

Lask looked after him, grateful, but worried.

Chapter Twenty-Nine

For days, Ari had been searching. She worked in her dreams from the moment she fell asleep until she opened her eyes the next morning, and though she slept soundly, she awoke exhausted. She called the names of the dragons across the great cosmic sea where all sleeping minds dream, but she found none of them. After a time, she changed her tactic, calling for any dragon who could hear her. She flung her mind out across the world in the night, searching farther than she knew the world could span. When she was beginning to think there were no dragons left, a sullen voice echoed back to her.

"Who is impudent enough to call for *dragons,* as if we have no names, and rude enough to intrude on a stranger's good night's sleep?"

Ari latched onto the voice and followed the thread of it, calling back,

"My name is Ari! Who are you? I have been searching for you every night."

"Why?" the voice answered. "Why should you care to find me?"

She was close to the source of the voice, and pursued it with her mind, sensing the other was making no move to approach her. At length, she found the voice's owner.

It was a dragon. Her heart leapt with joy. He was a serpentine red dragon, a variety she had never seen. He had no wings, and had bright gold horns like a stag. A thick golden mane grew around his head and down his back, all the way to the large flowing tail behind him. He regarded her with unimpressed gold eyes.

"Why, you are but a child," he growled. His head bowed lower to her, his eyes narrowing. "I have seen eyes like yours before. No one from this world could have eyes so bright and green. Answer me this, girl, are you kin to that snake Malachi?"

For a moment, Ari did not know how to answer, but she decided the dragon might know if she were lying, so replied,

"He is my great-uncle."

The dragon snorted a puff of smoke.

"You know him? How?"

"I sheltered the snake for over a decade," the dragon answered, "Until the day he left without so much as a goodbye or a thank you and stole what he could carry from my hoard. I called him a friend until that day. Long had he pestered me to help him return to the Gate, to Etheria. I told him again and again I would not; I had not left when Fah Ling asked, and I would not leave for him. I suppose he eventually realized I spoke truly, and thus I was of no more use to him."

"I am sorry," Ari said. She suspected the dragon did not exaggerate. "Who are you?"

"I suppose your wretched uncle would not have mentioned me." The golden whiskers on either side of his face twitched. "My name is Ajikhan. If you have business with me, speak it, else let me be. I've no interest in repeating the mistake I made long ago when I trusted the Immortal kind."

"I have sought you out to ask for your help, but not for me."

The dragon's hard expression softened a bit into mild curiosity.

"Do you know anything about the Mirror of Dùmsaro?"

Ajikhan's face darkened again.

"I do," he answered. "For even in the land that was meant to save them, my kind were hunted."

"It was imprisoned for millennia, but now my grandfather and his allies are trying to destroy it. It took one more dragon before it could be captured. Do you know any of the dragons it flung back to Earth? Ranseor or Adelina? Falsanthur?"

"Ranseor is dead," said Ajikhan, with no trace of pity. "He died below my mountains. I knew him, yes, and gave him succor. The fool was not content to hide like me, and went down to the village. They killed him. I suppose I should thank him, for they knew there was a dragon in these mountains, and when they killed him, they thought they'd gotten the last of them. I have not had to defend myself in many years. Nothing like folk thinking you're dead to secure your privacy."

"And the others?"

"Adelina is dead also," he answered, again with no note of sadness. "I heard the tale of her from an old monk I met some time ago. She tried to find the Gate back to your world and it was no longer there. Like a fool, in her despair, she inquired about it with the locals, and it was not long before a knight errant came to carve a reputation from her hide." He paused a moment, eyeing her. "This Falsanthur I have never heard of."

"Are there any other dragons left?"

"None that I know of. I never leave these mountains, but I used to have a handful of friends who would visit from time to time. They came less and less, and the last one I saw told me the others had gradually been tracked down and killed—either for trophies and novelties, or to destroy the evidence of our kind at last. Mankind thinks they are smart with their machines of smoke and steel, and their false stars in the sky they use like eyes. I daresay my last friend is dead too, for I have not seen her in over a hundred years."

"What year is it where I have found you?"

"Does it matter?" he asked, then confessed, "I do not know. I lost track long ago, and I do not keep time like Man does."

"There is another dragon left," Ari said, "For the Mirror has cast her to Earth just recently. She, too, spoke of smoking machines. Perhaps she is not far from you in time. I found her in dreams, as I have found you, and she asked me to seek out any dragons that were left."

"It would not surprise me if I am the last," said Ajikhan.

"Would you give her shelter if she came to you?"

The dragon scowled, and for a moment, Ari thought he would say no, but then:

"Yes. If she is no fool like the others, and could keep this place safe and unfound, then I would welcome her. These mountains are cold and lonely."

"Where are you?"

"Tell her to fly east. She will cross great deserts. Tell her to fly over the deserts until she comes to a sea, then follow the coast eastward, even if it should veer north or south; so long as she is flying east, she will be flying true. She will come to a river and must follow it inland. Follow it until it branches, then take the eastern most branch. When it branches again, take the south eastern branch. She must follow it into the mountains of black gravel. Just beyond the valley there are secluded peaks where few travel. It is there she will find me. Every night I will go out to one of them and release one bout of fire as a beacon."

"I will tell her," Ari said.

"What is her name?"

"Scoarin. She was the Hèadara of the dragons in Etheria."

"An aristocrat," grumbled Ajikhan, "Perfect..."

Ari reached out to him. He looked surprised, but did not pull away when she placed a hand on his forearm.

"Thank you," she said, "And I am sorry for the things Malachi did to you. He wronged many people, but has recently tried to make things right."

"Such does me little good," Ajikhan snorted, "And I care nothing about him. I shall wait for your friend Scoarin. That is all."

Chapter Thirty

Lask slept fitfully that night. He was awoken several times by the storm of emotions that thundered into his mind from Gonamadé's, distress and anguish, but as the night wore on, things seemed to change, and Lask could feel some deep, ancient power thrumming from the Gateway's mind. It was a profound feeling that brought a sense of awe to him, even though Lask did not fully know what it was.

He arose early, getting dressed without waking Myranda, and walked through the camp, out from the perimeter. He crossed the field, the spring wildflowers brushing against his legs, tugging at his cloak, moistening his boots with dew. Lask entered the forest, walking among the enormous, quiet trees, following the pull of Gonamadé's mind, until he at last came upon the Ancient.

The Gateway was sitting in a clearing atop a boulder, his fur catching the rising sunlight, outlining him in a warm glow. He was perfectly still, legs crossed and head bowed. The grass around the boulder was trampled and Lask saw deep scratches in the rock. From the now-blunted tips of the Gateway's golden claws, he realized the Ancient had torn at the rock in his distress.

Gonamadé did not seem to realize Lask was there. Lask watched him, seeing then the shape of something old as the world and powerful beyond measure. While Gonamadé was a joyful, warm companion, he was, too, one of the ancient powers that ruled the very course of history; old, mysterious, and greater than anyone knew.

Lask approached him with a sort of reverence, hearing the Gateway whispering in the Aetherian tongue. Lask could not understand him, but the quietness of his voice, the hushed, humble timbre of his words, made it obvious that he was praying. Lask was about to back away and leave him alone, when the Gateway whispered,

"Amén."

His blue eyes opened and caught sight of Lask, and his whole face pulled back into a broad grin.

"Oh!" he exclaimed. "Good morning!"

"Good morning," Lask answered, wary. "Are you alright?"

"Yes, I'm… I'm fine," said the Gateway, as if just realizing it himself. His grin widened by a few teeth. "I certainly do like it when Chai Karan is wrong."

"What—?"

"Last night was hard, certainly. I thought sure I was going to be— well, never mind that, but I had a very long discussion with the Creator and He said it was perfectly alright, that the Ancients were all bound to different degrees of silence and non-interference and He knew when He made me that I would have to be the freest of them." He paused to grin and shrug, saying, "Can't help myself, what can I say?" He gave a satisfied purr and continued, "Anyway, while I probably shouldn't go around saving *everyone* like I did last night, as that could prove problematic if it truly is someone's time to die, from now on, I'm going to help you whenever I want to!"

Lask listened to this rambling speech, a bit confused, but relieved nonetheless.

"You *spoke* to the Creator?" he asked, stunned.

"Well, yes, of course. All the Ancients can, though we don't as often as we used to. The First did too, your own great-grandfather included. Lu`corian was certainly an inquisitive fellow; it's just as well the One is enduringly patient." He grinned again and changed the subject, saying, "But yes. From now on, I'm not going to pay an ounce of attention to that pompous drokamerdor and I will help you however I can."

"That's excellent news."

"Isn't it?" Gonamadé leapt down off the rock and

grabbed Lask in a smothering furry hug.

Lask stiffened, surprised, and managed to free himself, drawing a grateful breath of air.

"I'm glad you are so happy," Lask remarked, turning to walk back toward the camp.

"Yes, it's quite nice," replied the Ancient, falling into step beside him. "I finally just decided to *ask* Him about something, and it's totally changed my outlook on things. I mean, I'd always *thought* surely it was true, but it's nice to have confirmation. Mystery will be thrilled. Chai Karan, of course, will not be happy at all."

Lask didn't know what the Ancient was talking about. He followed him as Gonamadé wandered into the camp and found Mystery. He approached her, taking her hands in his own with an eager, childlike grin to say,

"Guess what?"

"What?" asked Mystery, with a playful tone, as if humoring a small boy.

"I asked. You know, what everyone's been afraid to ask, because everyone was afraid of the answer."

"You did?" she said, stunned. "Well, what—"

"We do." Gonamadé grinned and nodded. "We all have souls. I knew we did. We *had* to."

Mystery gave an elated smile and flung her arms around the Gateway's furry neck. Lask himself couldn't help but smile at the two of them, so completely joyful they seemed. There was an impatient snort from nearby and they all looked to see Chai Karan had appeared.

"I've finished with the Merrus—"

"Chai Karan!" Mystery exclaimed. "Chai Karan, he asked!"

"What?" growled the drokamerdor.

Gonamadé sauntered in close to Time, draping an arm around his neck with a grin.

"I have been right all this time," said the Gateway. "You've been telling me I'm a fool, and as it turns out, that would be *you*."

"How dare you? You don't just *demand* to know things from the One—"

"Why not? The First did all the time. Besides, just because you ask, doesn't mean He's going to answer. But He did. And I think it's high time all of us knew for sure."

Chai Karan glowered at the Gateway.

"Oh, stop that," said Gonamadé. "You're just sour because now you actually have to act with some semblance of decency and start caring for that soul you've been denying all this time." The Gateway gave one of Chai Karan's whiskers a playful tug. Chai Karan snorted and shifted free of him.

The drokamerdor's nostrils flared and Lask could see him seething, fumbling for a response, but in the end, he just turned and stomped away.

"Chai Karan," Lask called after him.

The Ancient's head swung back to glare at him.

"You have gotten the answer from Lothanvar?"

"I have," replied Time. "I will need to create a way to capture the memory, as we must show it to him in order to properly banish him to Hell."

"Is there anything I can do to help you?"

"No." Chai Karan gave a sniff and trotted away.

"Don't mind him," said the Gateway. "Old stinker. He'll come around."

Chapter Thirty-One

Calliban's whipping wings had flung them over the kingdom, shooting through the air like a dark comet. They had passed the Fairy force long ago, and had soared high above them out of sight, the dark dragon invisible against the night sky. Forge hunkered down on his back against the stinging wind as they flew. The air was cold so high up and the general wrapped his cloak tighter around himself, wishing he'd brought a coat as well.

The dragon was the fastest member of the Kyn, and Forge admired his stamina. The young dragon whizzed over the Plains without stopping, traveling through the night and into the morning. It was noon of the following day when Calliban tucked his wings to land on a peak in the great mountainous wall of the Therakas, which surrounded the Barren Region. The dragon was gasping, saying,

"Just a little rest, then we'll go on."

Forge slid from his back, patting his side.

"Sleep for a few hours if you like," the general told him. "You've gotten us here far faster than anyone thought you would."

The exhausted dragon flopped out on his side, glad to oblige, spreading his wings out over the ground on either side of him to soak in the sunlight. Forge kept watch while he rested, though there was no one around for miles. When mid-afternoon came, the general roused the dragon and they continued on, soaring out over the vast expanse of the desert.

Calliban banked further south, turning toward the most commonly traveled route in the Barren Region. Sure enough, his sharp eyes picked out tracks. He pointed them out to the general and quickened his pace, following them over the hard, sun-baked ground, until he came to an abrupt halt.

"Land!" Forge exclaimed. "Go!"

Calliban obliged, as he could see no hydras in the empty space around them. He tucked his wings and dove down to the grisly sight below.

All ten of the soldiers that had escorted Fiora lay dead in the dust, some crushed, some gutted, and some in pieces. The thirsty ground drank in their blood, sapping the moisture out of them under the hot sun. Calliban gagged, and Forge brought a hand to his mouth, disgusted and horrified. All of their horses had suffered the same fate, lying broken and torn in the dirt. Fiora's golden mare was among them.

"We're too late," said Calliban.

"Fiora isn't here," Forge said, "They have taken her. Cazour wouldn't kill one of the nobles; she's too valuable to just kill and leave out here." He turned back to the dragon, pulling himself back up onto Calliban's shoulders. "Come, we must return to the United as fast as we can to mount a rescue."

Chapter Thirty-Two

When Ari found Scoarin again, she told the dragon of Ajikhan and relayed the directions Ajikhan had given her. Scoarin managed a faint smile and said,

"I am very grateful to you, Ariana, though it saddens me to hear of poor Ranseor and Adelina."

"I will keep looking for Falsanthur," she promised. "Perhaps he may still be alive." She paused and studied Scoarin's sad face. "I could probably bring you to Calliban in these dreams," she said.

"No," Scoarin answered, quickly and almost snapping. "No, it would be too painful. Better for him to think of me as dead for now. I fear what little heart I have left would break at the sight of him, knowing I will never touch his face again."

"Is there anyone you would like to see? My father? My grandfather? The Gateway?"

"No, child," said the dragon. "For my days in Etheria are done, and I do not wish to torture myself by keeping company with memories." She bowed her head, then wrapped her tail around Ari. "Thank you for finding me. At least if I can find this Ajikhan, I will not be alone. Perhaps, at the very least, we might pass out of the world together."

Chapter Thirty-Three

It was evening of the following day when an exhausted Calliban landed on the perimeter. The dragon collapsed on the ground where he landed, panting, and Forge slid from his back, calling for water to be brought for the dragon. Lask came to the edge of the camp, having seen the dragon's approach. Forge shook his head.

"We were too late," he said. "The hydras have killed all ten soldiers that accompanied her and, as best as I can tell, have taken Fiora hostage."

"Damn it all," Lask growled. "How long has it been?"

"The kills were fresh, no more than a few hours old. Given the time it took us to get back, I'd say she's been their prisoner for about two days."

"Cazour hasn't sent anything demanding a ransom."

"Might not have gotten here yet."

"We must go after her. Go and rest. I will inform the

council."

Forge gave a grateful nod. Lask had several of the guards on the perimeter run to gather the leaders of the races. As they did so, Lask walked through the camp to the meeting place, and Myranda came to walk alongside him, knowing immediately that something was wrong.

"What is it?" she asked.

"The Hydras have Fiora."

Myranda glanced up at him, seeing the tightness of his jaw, and knew he feared for her. While they had long since gone their separate ways, Lask had once courted Fiora, and Myranda knew that even for Immortals, that spark of youthful affection would always endure on some level. Myranda reached down to take his hand.

"She'll be alright," she said. "The Hydras wouldn't kill someone so valuable."

"Let us hope you are right."

Chapter Thirty-Four

The council was already in a rage when Lask arrived. Polian was bellowing incoherent vows of vengeance upon Julius, brandishing his axe skyward in the direction the Fairies had gone. Vatron was crouched as if to spring, smoke curling from her nostrils. Ossifer and Morpheus's necks were both indistinguishable from their heads, so bristled were their hackles. The moranters' claws were buried up to their knuckles in the ground. Even Rosecca, normally the pacifist, was snorting and stamping at the ground.

"This is war!" roared Polian upon Lask's approach. "As if it were not enough the Fairies have left us, their allies have kidnapped the Elinsara. I say we rally right now and set off; crush them on the battlefield within a week."

"We are not prepared to launch a full scale war yet," Lask replied. "We're only just recovering from Vortearigan. We will need to gather the necessary supplies, to call in the rest of the army—"

"Surely you do not intend to let the Hydras and the Fairies go unanswered for so long!" crowed Ossifer. "If the hydras' attack on us and Fiora's kidnapping are not acts of war—"

"They are," said Lask, "But right now, we cannot afford to rush into anything. We must first and foremost focus on destroying the Mirror and Lothanvar before we turn our attention to the Hydras. Chai Karan has found what he needs from the Merrus and is preparing a means to use it. Let us hope it is finished quickly and let us do anything we can to help the Ancients. Ossifer, you and your griffins can begin regular scouting of the Hydras and the Fairies. Make sure they are not moving to attack anything and estimate their numbers and resources as best you can. Once we have finished with the Mirror we will decide what to do about Cazour and Julius—"

"Kill them!" bellowed Polian, "That's what we need to do! No debate needed."

The council snarled their approval.

"In the meantime," Lask said, with a pointed glance at the all-too-eager centaur, "I will lead a small, covert mission to rescue Fiora. I plan on asking the Gateway if he could provide us with any concealing magic."

Chapter Thirty-Five

"Certainly I can give you an invisibility spell," said Gonamadé upon Lask's query, "But it won't do you much good."

"Why not?" Lask asked.

"Because the Hydra fortress is just that: it's impenetrable unless they let you in. Everything is enormous. There'd be no way to sneak in a side door unnoticed even if you could open it."

"So how do you propose we get in then?"

"A decoy," said Forge, who'd been listening in. "All we'd need is one person to get them to open the door, and the rest of us sneak in under the invisibility spell."

"I know you are a master of disguise, my friend," Lask answered, "But I think passing one of us off as a hydra is beyond even your skill."

"We don't need to pretend to be hydras," replied Forge with a crafty grin. "Not when they're allied with the

Fairies."

Lask caught on and the Gateway smiled in approval.

"I could probably enchant you a pair of convincing wings," said the Ancient, "They wouldn't be able to fly and you wouldn't want anyone to touch them, but they'd be convincing to look at."

"Do you think we could get in and back out that way?" Forge asked, hopeful.

"If we cast the right fairy," Lask replied with a sly smile.

Chapter Thirty-Six

"No." Malachi looked outraged. "I draw the line at impersonating fairies!"

"If there's anyone who can talk his way in and out of the Hydra stronghold it's *you*," Lask replied.

"You'll all be invisible. If anything goes wrong, *I'll* be the one getting his head snapped off!"

Lask shrugged, as if suggesting this would not be any great loss. Malachi scoffed, but was not surprised.

"Fine," he said, "Let's say I agree to do this. How am I going to walk right out the front door of the castle with Fiora?"

"Working on that," said the Gateway from nearby. He held up a plain, silver ring that he'd been enchanting with the invisibility magic. "You'll all just need to wear one of these for the magic to work. I'll make an extra for Fiora. Don't put them on until you have to though. I can't promise that the magic will last much longer than four or five hours."

"What about footprints?" Malachi asked, determined to punch a hole in their plan. "It's a desert. They're bound to see the extra footprints in the dust."

Lask exchanged a glance with Gonamadé, neither of them having thought of that.

"We'll just have to wear soft shoes and tread lightly, I suppose," Lask said.

Malachi gave a dissatisfied grunt.

"And if I run into another fairy?" he asked. "Surely they'll recognize I'm not one of them. I *am* awfully tall for a fairy."

"You've always been an excellent liar," Lask replied.

Malachi just gave him a look and muttered a grudging agreement.

Chapter Thirty-Seven

The next morning, Lask, Myranda, Forge and Malachi met Calliban on the outskirts of the camp to set out to the Barren Region. Before they left, Gonamadé came to meet them to place his magic on Malachi.

"What color wings would you like?" asked the Ancient, seeming delighted at the prospect. "Shall I make them sort of long and pointed, or broad and squarish?"

"I don't give a damn, just do it," Malachi muttered, still not at all pleased about the notion.

"I suppose I'll just take some creative liberties then."

Gonamadé grabbed him by the shoulders and spun him around to get a better view of his back. Malachi grudgingly obliged and stood still. Gonamadé eyed him for a moment, then nodded to himself and rubbed his hands together. He prodded him in the shoulders and slowly worked his hands back, leaving planes of light in their wake. The Gateway pulled and rubbed at the light sculpting it into the shape of graceful wings. Once he had shaped them, he snapped his fingers and the light solidified into a pair of green spotted wings, which even carried the slight shimmer of real fairy wings. Everyone present was impressed, even the skeptical Malachi. Forge reached out to touch them, amazed, only to have his hand pass through.

"That's why you don't want anyone to touch them," said the Gateway.

"And how long will this magic last?" inquired Lask. "It will take us at least a day if not more to fly to the Barren Region, and that's if Calliban flies at a sprint as he did before."

"They should last days, maybe even weeks," Gonamadé replied. "Illusions like this are extremely easy magic; even people with very little magic can preserve a convincing illusion for several hours. Being an Ancient, I'm confident mine will last a week at least." He gave a satisfied grin. "I'll probably have to take them off when you return. Unless you'd like to start a new fashion, Malachi."

Malachi glared at him.

"Perhaps not, then," said the Gateway. "Best of luck to all of you. I wish I could accompany you, but the Ancients dare not leave the Mirror, especially not since Chai

Karan has confirmed it's sharing power with Lothanvar. I probably shouldn't linger away from the cave much longer as it is."

Chapter Thirty-Eight

"I am pleased to see you here, fairy," rumbled the Hydra King. "I was beginning to wonder if you were going to keep our agreement."

"I shall and I have," replied Julius.

"What is this grave look on your face?" Cazour inquired. "Are you not pleased to be called my ally?"

"I would be more pleased if my own kind were unified in our decision."

"You are not?" Cazour looked down at him with dissatisfied eyes.

"There is one who is sowing dissent. He did not agree with our joining you from the start and I fear he is swaying the others to agree with him. He might even be able to lead a mutiny—"

"Then why do you not silence him?" Cazour demanded. "There is but one way to deal with dissenters and keep one's power secure."

"I wish it were that simple, but—"

"It is always that simple," growled the hydra.

"But he is my second," said Julius, "The one I have known since birth, who I have always counted as my brother. He may well be the only friend I have."

"If he would stand against you, he is not your friend, only an obstacle."

Julius was silent and glanced down to the tiled floor.

"You must deal with this dissenter," commanded the hydra, "Consider it the first test of your loyalty. Silence him, but do not only that; make an example of him. Let his be the name that stands for what happens to our enemies and those who would stand in our way. Do not give him the mercy of a clean execution. *Destroy him*. Perhaps then your kind will know my power and yours."

Chapter Thirty-Nine

Fiora was working her way through reading the large pile of letters that she'd let grow on her desk a bit longer than she should have. She had made decent progress, but it was getting to the point where her mind refused to focus any longer. Her eyes began to imagine the letters dancing on the page, swimming over the paper and rearranging themselves.

There was a merciful knock at the door. As she'd locked it earlier to avoid being disturbed, she got up and crossed the chamber. When she unlocked it and pulled the door open she found a most welcome sight. The smell of the colorful array of flowers hit her immediately when she opened the door. Their vibrant colors seemed to glow after her eyes had had nothing to look at but black letters for hours.

"You are such a dear," she said, taking them.

"You've been in here all day," Lask replied. "You haven't even eaten."

"Oh!" Fiora exclaimed, face awash in sudden guilt. "Oh, I was supposed to meet you for lunch."

"Yes," answered Lask. He produced a basket. "But you should know I'm not that easy to avoid."

Fiora smiled and led him inside. Lask crossed the room and set the basket of food on the only clear corner of her desk, pulling up an extra chair for himself, remarking,

"I suppose the Senate will be glad to know you still put your work above *me*."

"Did Falana send you an angry letter too?"

"She's only ever sent me angry letters, starting from the first week I came to office," Lask replied. "Although I'm sorry to hear she's apparently bothering you with them."

Fiora fished through the pile of letters on the desk and produced one that Lask recognized to be in the sharp, hurried script of his least favorite senator.

"I wish I could be as dismissive of her as you are," Fiora murmured, sinking into her chair across from him. She accepted the bread he offered her. "She's proven to be noisy and a bully. What if she starts getting the others riled?"

"There's nothing that says two members of the noble lines can't be romantic with one another."

"But it's never happened before."

"All the more reason for it to happen," Lask replied with a crooked smile.

Fiora shook her head. Lask reached out and took her face in his hand.

"I have no qualms about the idea," he said. "As long as you don't either, that's all the more approval I need."

Fiora smiled at him and tossed Falana's letter aside.

Chapter Forty

For being in a hot desert, the dungeon of the Hydra fortress was cold. Fiora felt tiny in the cell; the door was enormous and the window was far too high for her to see out of, unless one of the hydras walked directly past. It was grimy and dusty, and it was a long time before Fiora was tired enough to sit on the filthy floor. Her attackers had dragged her in before Cazour, who had done little more than gloat over her capture and have her thrown in the dungeon, but Fiora imagined there would be more to come.

In the grungy gloom, she found her thoughts wandering not to her friends, her sister, or her husband. Rather, her mind settled on and clutched at the thought of Lask, wondering what he was doing, if he was worried about her. Surely he was already planning her rescue.

Though she had ended their youthful romance of several years because of all the political questions and turmoil that surrounded it, she sometimes found herself wishing that she could still wrap herself up in those strong arms; there was no safer place in all the world.

Just then, a hydra appeared at the door, a visibly old female, with wiry silver hairs sprouting from her ears. She wore a gold ring in the right ear of her dominant head. Her yellow eyes were bulbous and her necks were skinny. The skin of her throats sagged. Two of her heads worked to unlock the door and she came inside, pushing the door shut behind her.

"What a pleasure to meet you, Elinsara," said Syringa, though her scratchy voice was patronizing and sarcastic.

Fiora was silent, standing there, cornered against the wall. She knew she was no match for this beast and there was no way she could open the immense door by herself, even if it was unlocked.

"We hydras are too large to be good spies, as you can imagine," said Syringa, "So we're going to need some information from you. The fairy gave us a fair amount, but Cazour wishes to know what you can tell us."

"Nothing," Fiora replied, staunch and unwavering under the hydra's glaring eyes. "I would gladly discuss the Hydras' relations to the rest of the kingdom with your king, but I will give him nothing that would support his treason."

"Treason," crooned Syringa, "It's all matter of perspective. When Cazour makes his war and becomes king of all of you, you will have been the traitor for denying him."

"I hold my power in this kingdom by blood and divine right," Fiora replied. "Your king cannot in any way lay claim to that."

"Julius was certainly right about the arrogance of you aristocrats," muttered Syringa. "Well," she said, "I was going to bring you some supper, but if you insist on being so uppity and uncooperative, I'll just have to starve you."

"I will not be here long," Fiora told her. "You have kidnapped a noble of the realm. Our Protector will not stand for it."

"Cazour certainly hopes he won't. The Hydra King looks forward to the war your Somadar shall wage on him."

Chapter Forty-One

When Julius returned from the Hydra castle, he found Sutonius waiting for him on the edge of the camp. The other fairy's orange wings were held rigid and he did not move when Julius came stalking in close to him.

"We must speak of this," Sutonius told him, "There are others as well who wish me to speak to you. This was never—"

"Be silent," Julius snarled. "If you do not still that dissenting tongue, you shall force me to do it for you."

"Is that what it's come to?" asked Sutonius. "I, who am your brother by the sword and the wing, cannot even bring you to your senses? Surely you see what has happened. You have let your own pride dig you into this mire and now it is fear that shall keep you trapped in what can only end in our doom. Think of the rest of us, of all those in Finistrì. You have made all of them the United's enemy, and as one who fought beside them, you surely know what becomes of their enemies!"

"Do not force me to silence you," Julius said, and Sutonius could not tell if it was a threat or plea.

"Someone must break the silence," Sutonius replied, "And I will no longer be afraid to do it. If you will not be strong as our race needs you to be, then I will."

Julius stood there across from him, silent, his blue eyes locked with Sutonius's hazel ones, each studying the other, begging, threatening, daring. Julius's eyes flicked over to the guards on the perimeter and he snapped,

"Seize him and bind him."

"Julius—" Sutonius protested.

Julius shoved past him, ignoring him as the soldiers grabbed hold of his friend, stalking away into the camp. The soldiers dragged Sutonius to the center of camp, struggling against his kicking feet and flailing wings, to where they started to yank his arms up to tie him to a post there, but Julius, returning, said,

"No. The other way."

The soldiers obeyed, wrestling the still struggling Sutonius around to tie him facing the post, leaving his back and wings exposed. The soldiers glanced to the waiting general, who nodded for them to unbutton the back of the prisoner's shirt. Sutonius felt the hot rays of the sun meet his bare skin and he looked over his shoulder to see

Julius standing behind him. His eyes were drawn to a movement of the other fairy's hands and he looked down to see Julius unrolling a whip.

"Is this it then, brother?" he asked, quiet.

Julius said nothing, planting his feet in a steadying stance.

"You've always been reckless," said Sutonius, "I suppose I should have known there would come a day when I could not talk you out of it. You have never been kind, but I did not believe you to be cruel."

Still Julius said nothing, getting a grip on the handle of the whip.

"You don't have to be afraid," Sutonius told him, "The Hydra King does not hold nearly the power you think he does. We could have left this awful place together, made our peace with our brethren." He looked at his friend, seeing no trace of the man he once knew. "And though you now repay my years of loyalty and honest friendship with bitter betrayal, know that even now, I do not hate you."

Julius drew back his arm and Sutonius turned his head away. There was a crack and a sickening tearing sound. Julius stood there, clutching the whip, looking at the line of shimmering crimson blood welling up on his friend's shoulder and the long tear along his left wing, the torn edges beading with blood.

The camp had fallen into a frozen hush and Julius glanced to the side, seeing horrified, frightened faces, then looked back at the dark fortress behind him. On all sides was the bleak, barren nothingness he had brought them to, and the vulnerable, resolute, form of Sutonius waited before him.

He drew back his arm and another crack broke the silence. He heard Sutonius's breath catch. Another crack, another tear. It became a grim rhythm, the snapping and the shredding. Sutonius stood there, head bowed against the post. Blood trickled in glistening rivers down the curve of his back and the planes of his wings, slicking their shimmering dust, dripping onto the barren ground.

The worst part was the sound. There were many who turned away, unable to watch the mutilation of their comrade, but clenched eyes could not defend them from the awful ripping of the whip as it tore through once proud wings. Sutonius did his best to stay quiet, but his breath had become ragged gasping, and the sight-blurring agony sapped the strength from him, until he could stand no more, only hang from his bonds, slumped against the post. And as the pieces of his wings began fall like mortal leaves, littering the dust around him, Julius drew from him a hollow, forsaken cry that brought cringes to the faces of all who had not already fled the hellish scene.

There was so much blood when Julius finally

stopped. The sputtering, trembling form of Sutonius was drenched in it and the ravenous ground drank in what would have been a pool of it around him, a gruesome halo outlining him as he hung, broken amid the fallen tatters of his wings, and his gasping breath was the only sound in the desolate silence.

"Cut him down," Julius told his soldiers, cold voice cutting through the frozen scene, "And drag him into the desert. Let the sun and the dust have him."

The soldiers obeyed, cutting through the ropes and letting the ruined form of Sutonius crumple into the dust and the blood. They reached for him, hands slipping on his blood-slicked skin as they got a hold on his arms, hauling him through the camp and out past the perimeter. His hollow, rasping breath seemed to be in eerie harmony with the scraping of his legs over the hardened, dusty ground as they dragged him out into the scorching wasteland. When they were almost out of sight of the camp, they let go, letting him fall into a tattered mass among the dust, leaving him to die under the searing eye of the sun.

Chapter Forty-Two

Maléchian glanced at the two Ancients sitting across the cavern from him, and to the other, Chai Karan, who was pacing just outside. The drokamerdor was talking to Socadan, organizing the materials needed to make some kind of magical artifact. Since the Mirror's connection to Lothanvar had been discovered, all three of the Ancients had been keeping vigil over the prisoners, not leaving for anything, as Ancients did not even need to eat or sleep, but only did so for pleasure.

They've done something wrong, you know, the Mirror remarked to Lothanvar, communicating telepathically to avoid detection by the Ancients.

What do you mean? Lothanvar growled, not looking at Maléchian so not to appear suspicious.

This magic that's holding me is not as strong as it was before when they locked me away. What's holding you is cer-

tainly not as strong as it should be. They used a few different ingredients, and not enough, I think. I've been wearing away at mine. If I could get free, I could free you.

So do it, then.

I said their magic was weaker, not that I could break through it yet. Perhaps if you lend me some strength I could get through it faster.

Lothanvar said nothing, but Maléchian felt a surge of power rush into him from his maker. The Mirror soaked it in, reveling in it, and tore away at the Ancients' magic, sure it would not be much longer.

Chapter Forty-Three

Calliban had once more done an admirable job of reaching the Barren Region in a little over a day's time. It was late afternoon when they arrived. Lask commended the dragon for his stamina, and promised him a week's undisturbed rest when they returned. The dragon landed in the midst of the desert, just out of sight of the Hydra fortress. They had flown over it, seeing the Fairies' camp beyond and had been sure to land far on the south side to avoid detection from any flying fairy messengers.

Calliban, Myranda and Lask kept watch while Forge began preparations to disguise Malachi. As he was mixing the paints, Malachi changed into the fairy uniform that he'd brought, one that had been left behind in the camp when the fairies deserted. It was not a very good fit; too baggy for his lanky frame, and also too short for his long torso, but it would have to do. Myranda had to help him button it at the back around the wings, Malachi muttering that he didn't know how the Fairies managed to get dressed every day.

Forge came after him with a paintbrush and Malachi craned his head away, only to receive a smack on the back of the head from Lask. Grumbling, he sat still and let Forge paint a creamy complexion over his chalky white skin. The general was very good at his work, taking great care to properly shade the cheeks and around the eyes, even taking up a tiny fine brush to dot a few freckles across the bridge of Malachi's pointy nose.

"This paint itches," Malachi groused. "I think you got it in my eye."

"I'll put the whole brush in your eye if you don't stop complaining," Forge retorted.

When at last the disguise was complete, Forge stepped back to consider his work.

"I'd believe it," remarked Calliban.

"You make quite the handsome fairy, Malachi," Lask said.

Malachi just glared at him and started trudging off in the direction of the Hydra castle without another word. The others joined him, leaving Calliban to hide and rest. As they drew nearer to the fortress, they slipped the enchanted rings onto their fingers, so that it appeared Malachi walked alone. They quickened their pace so to not waste the magic, but it was still a long way to the fortress.

When they arrived, Malachi sauntered up to the gate to approach the guards there. The other three tread behind him, as light and quiet as they could, hoping the hydras would not notice any extra tracks.

"What do you want, fairy?" growled one of the hydras.

"Message from Julius for the Hydra King," replied Malachi.

"Leave it here, then."

"He insisted I deliver it in person. Besides, I doubt you'd remember it all. It's quite a long message and boring; reports from Finistrì, supply requests, political questions—"

"Fine, just go," snapped the hydra, impatient. "Go straight down the main hall and don't tarry."

"And don't get stepped on, insect," jeered the other guard, pushing the door open for him.

Malachi gave him a nod of thanks and passed inside, taking a slow, strolling pace (much to the hydras' annoyance) so the others had time to get past.

"Do you suppose they're keeping her in the dungeon?" whispered Forge.

"Never mind the dungeon," hissed Malachi from the corner of his mouth. He sniffed at the air, then took a sharp turn down a right corridor. "Kitchen must be this way."

"The kitchen?" whispered Lask. "This is no time for—"

"You of all people should have faith in my scheming, brother," growled Malachi.

They made their way down the vast corridor, creeping under the glaring eyes of passing hydras. Sure enough, they came into a wide dining hall where food was being prepared over an open fire at the far end. The others crowded in around Malachi as he walked, not wanting to be hit by one of the many hydras milling about the room. Malachi sauntered up to one of the hydras preparing the afternoon meal.

"What do you want?" growled the hydra. "Don't expect me to feed you. You lot are supposed to be supplying yourselves."

"I'm Julius's interrogator," Malachi replied. "Word is your king is having a hard time getting anything useful out of his noble prisoner and Julius volunteered my services."

"What's that got to do with me?" the hydra snarled.

"I'd like to take her a small bit of supper. After being hungry for so long, I'm sure food will be a good incentive for her to cooperate. And if not, well, there are other ways." He gave the hydra that sinister smirk that Lask was all too familiar with.

The hydra gave a rumbling chuckle and reached over with one of his heads to tear off a bit of roasting meat to offer the fairy.

"Much obliged," Malachi replied. He started to walk away, then paused, turning back to ask, "She is still being held in the dungeon, isn't she? Cazour hasn't had her brought up yet?"

"She's still down there as far as I know," rumbled the hydra.

Malachi nodded and wandered back out into the corridor, the others following close behind him. They went back out to the main hall and followed it down to the end. Malachi's shrewd eyes noticed the guards at the tall doors that could only lead to the throne room, and another guard standing by an archway off to the side. He walked straight for the archway and was about to walk past the hydra, when the guard stopped him, lowing a single head to hiss at him.

"Where do you think you're going?"

"I'm supposed to be interrogating the prisoner. I'm already late. So if you don't mind, I can't exactly afford any more delays."

The hydra made an irritated noise, but nonetheless moved aside. Malachi went past him, only to find himself standing at the top of an enormous set of stairs. It was easily a four foot drop down to the next one.

"Mind yourselves," he hissed to the others behind him and leapt down to the next step.

The others slid down, trying to ease themselves down and muffle the sound of their feet as much as possible. It was still a little too noisy for Malachi's liking. One of the guard's heads swiveled back to eye him.

"What's the point in having those wings if you can't even use them to get down to the dungeon?" sneered the hydra.

"It's impolite to fly indoors!" Malachi retorted without missing a beat.

The hydra snorted and turned back around muttering,

"Fairies..."

Malachi picked his way down the steps, the others lowering themselves after him, praying another hydra wouldn't be coming up from below. When they reached the bottom, Malachi turned to look back at the staircase, shaking his head.

"There's no way we're going to be able to get back up there fast enough and quiet enough, and with Fiora in tow, especially if she is wounded."

"We don't have much choice," Lask whispered.

Malachi set off down the hallway, having to bend down and look under the cell doors to see inside, as the barred windows were far too high to see through. Most of the cells were empty. Malachi guessed the Hydras had a simple legal system; either the prisoner was released or killed. There was only one hydra in the cells that they passed, a creature looking so starved and frail, there would be no need to worry about him seeing them pass. Finally, Malachi looked into a cell near the end of the hall and spied a pair of dust-coated human shoes in the corner.

He stood up and pulled out his knife, having to stand on tiptoe and reach over his head to finagle the lock. It was a huge, iron mechanism, and Malachi worried he might break the tip of his dagger before it would let go. While the blade did emerge bent, the lock snapped open. Malachi hefted it off, Lask reaching up to help him set it down so that it would not clang onto the floor. It took all four of them to shove the immense cell door open.

Fiora was backed into the corner and looked startled to see a fairy there.

"Who are you?" she demanded.

"It's just Malachi."

"Lask?" she asked, surprised and knowing his voice.

She felt a long-fingered hand close over hers.

"There's not much time to explain," he said. "The Gateway has enchanted these rings, which will keep us invisible for a few hours."

She felt him slip cold metal onto her finger, and as

soon as it was in place, she could see his faded shape, and those of Myranda and Forge behind him. She flung her arms around him, the mask of noble strength slipping away for a moment, as she whispered,

"I knew you would come for me."

"I always will," Lask told her, returning her embrace for a moment. "Come, we must go. We have a long climb to make."

She released him, shaking her head.

"We'll never be able to make it back up that staircase undetected."

"That's what I said," Malachi muttered.

"There might be another way out," said Fiora. "That other hydra, Aldebaran, came down to look in on me several times. More than once I saw him continue down the hall and not return."

"It's worth a look."

They filed back out into the hallway and continued down it. There was another door at the end. It was unlocked and they heaved it open to find themselves in a vast cellar. There were piles upon piles of salted meat and dry, brittle grass, stacked amid towering barrels. Fiora stood up on tiptoe, looking across the room and pointed.

"There!"

Sure enough, there was a set of stairs carved into the hard dirt walls, leading to some kind of enormous hatch.

"Will we be able to lift that?" asked Forge.

"Only one way to know," Lask replied, heading for the stairs.

They hauled themselves up, Lask having to reach back and help pull Fiora up as she started to tire towards the top. Lask, Forge and Malachi braced themselves against the hatch and shoved it upwards, managing to raise it up by a few feet.

"Go," Lask grunted to Myranda and Fiora.

The two women pulled themselves up and slipped out under the edge of the hatch. Myranda got a hold on the lip of it once she was outside, taking off a little of the weight. Fiora followed suit.

"One of you come up," said Myranda.

Forge nodded to Lask and Lask let go, hauling himself out onto the dusty ground beyond. He bent down to help hold the hatch so Forge could let go and climb out. The general too got a hold on the door, remarking with a crooked grin,

"We could just leave him in there."

"I heard that," Malachi growled, crawling out after them.

He stood up and dusted himself off. They had emerged at the back of the stronghold. Malachi glanced up and immediately plastered himself back against the wall, motioning for the others to shut the hatch. They did so and looked up, seeing a hydra guard patrolling the ramparts high above. Malachi edged his way along the wall keeping himself pressed up tight against the stone to remain out of view. The others tiptoed along with him, and Fiora whispered to Lask,

"Two guards came down into the dungeon earlier today, bringing food for me and the other prisoners. They were talking to one another about the Fairies. One of them said Julius had been having problems with his second and that he had to silence him to stop a mutiny. I fear something terrible has happened to Sutonius. How much longer will your invisibility magic last?"

"Another hour, maybe two," Lask hissed back. "Though I don't want to risk going into the fairy camp like this."

They had reached the end of the wall, and Malachi sauntered away as if he were heading back to the Fairy camp, though angled his path as he walked to swing away from it. Thankfully, the Fairies had kept a good distance from the Hydra fortress, so it was possible to walk out into the desert between the two with a good chance neither race would be looking hard enough to notice. As they walked back toward the place Calliban would be waiting, Myranda nudged Lask and pointed off into the distance. Lask followed her gaze, spotting a small shape in the distance, disrupting the flat void of the desert.

"What is that?" she asked.

"I don't know," Lask replied. He nodded to Forge. "Come with me. The rest of you go on ahead and find Calliban. We'll catch up to you shortly."

They parted ways and Lask and Forge struck off across the barren plain toward it. As they drew closer, Lask realized what it was.

He rushed toward the crumpled form, Forge close behind him. Sutonius lay face down in the dust, the tatters of his wings slumped onto the ground on either side of him, pieces of them having fallen off entirely, lying around him like crumpled pages torn from a book. The copper-spotted skin of his back was streaked with countless lashes, most still open.

"That bastard," Forge growled.

Lask knelt beside the fairy, thinking he must surely be dead, and raised his head up out of the dust, holding a pale hand under his nose. To his complete surprise, the faint breeze of shallow breath passed over his fingers.

"He's alive!" Lask exclaimed.

"How—?"

"Here, help me."

Lask took one of the fairy's arms, pulling him up. Forge went to his other side and the two hefted the battered form of Sutonius between them, dragging him back toward the place where the others waited. As they walked, Sutonius's feet dragging through the dust behind them, Lask reached out to Gonamadé in his mind.

Lask? came the Gateway's voice, *What is it?*

You must come, Lask told him, *Sutonius has been terribly hurt. I am amazed he's still alive. We must get him to Salìt NOW. I fear he will not make it if we must travel all the way back.*

But we have to keep guard on Lothanvar. If one of us leaves, they might—

Might, Lask replied, *Something MIGHT happen. If you do not come to get us, it is CERTAIN Sutonius will die.*

Alright, said the Gateway, *I'm coming.*

Lask and Forge continued on toward Calliban, and in a few moments there was a flash of gold light and the Gateway appeared nearby.

"Very subtle," Lask muttered. "I'm sure someone saw that. We should be away quickly."

"Oh dear," said Gonamadé, looking at Sutonius.

"Can you do anything?" Lask asked as they approached the others.

"Afraid it wouldn't do much good," the Gateway replied. "I can't fix what's no longer there, and he's been like this for a few hours I'd wager. If I healed everything now, so quickly with magic, he'd scar terribly, possibly bad enough to hinder his motion in the future."

Fiora gasped at the sight of the fairy and Myranda brought a hand to her mouth.

"Alright, everyone, gather round," said the Gateway.

They all crowded in around the Ancient and Gonamadé raised his hands. A prickling sensation washed over them and everything seemed to lurch. Lask felt his stomach drop as the magic yanked them out of the Barren Region and whisked them away back to the north.

Chapter Forty-Four

T*he cat is gone. It's now or never!* growled Lothanvar.

Maléchian had already come to that conclusion. With a final push, he snapped the cords of magic binding him fast. Mystery was on her feet in an instant, golden light pouring from her palms as she screamed,

"Chai Karan!"

The Mirror silenced her with a bolt of green light, blasting her backwards. Wasting no time, Maléchian sent his magic at Lothanvar, tearing at the cords that bound the Merrus. Lothanvar exerted his own magic, black muscles straining, as Chai Karan came galloping into the cavern. The final bonds of the Ancients' magic snapped under Lothanvar's struggles and the Merrus billowed up toward the cavern ceiling to avoid the magic Chai Karan hurled at him. Lothanvar flung a bolt of red light down at the drokamerdor and Chai Karan deflected it with his own magic. Before the Ancient could strike again, there was a crash like thunder and a blinding flash of green light.

"NO!" Chai Karan roared.

The Mirror and Lothanvar were gone.

Chapter Forty-Five

When Gonamadé's magic deposited them on the outskirts of the camp, Chai Karan came galloping up to them, growling, "This is *your* fault!"

Lask and the Gateway both blinked, not sure who was being addressed.

"*Yours,*" Time snarled at Lask, "For using the precious Spring water to heal a griffin and calling away the Gateway, again endangering everything for the sake of one creature, and *yours,*" he snapped at the Gateway, "For leaving!"

"What are you talking about?" asked Gonamadé.

"The Mirror and Lothanvar! They've escaped!"

"*What?*" chorused everyone present.

"Inform the council," Lask said, gathering his wits, "We will meet with the Ancients within the hour. In the meantime, we have to get Sutonius to the healers."

The others disbanded to find the other leaders, while Lask and Forge carried Sutonius into the camp.

"Salìt!" Lask called to his soldiers. "Find Salìt!"

He and Forge hauled Sutonius towards the center of camp to the healers' tent. Salìt came running up as they arrived, helping them inside.

"Lay him here," said the physician.

When Sutonius had been laid out on one of the low beds, Salìt sat down beside him, looking over the fairy.

"Damn," he murmured, a note of amazed sorrow in his voice. He waved over two of the healers, who brought poultices and cleansing wine. They started their work, wiping away the dried blood that had caked on his back and wings. It was a horrific mess, and Salìt exchanged a look with the two other healers. They knew what needed done, but no one seemed to have the heart to do it. Salìt steeled himself, and took up one of his surgical knives and started cutting away the worst of the tatters, leaving as much of the wing as he could, shearing off the pieces that were beyond repair. He passed the pieces, grim faced, over into the large bowl one of the other healers held for him.

"Is there any hope for him?" Lask asked as he watched, breaking the heavy silence.

"I can save his life," replied Salìt, "But he will never fly again."

Lask nodded and stepped outside, making his way to where the council was gathering, Forge following in his wake. It didn't take long for everyone to assemble.

"You lost the Mirror?" Ossifer squawked to Chai Karan.

"Not by any fault of mine," snarled Time.

"It doesn't matter whose fault it is," said Vatron. "We must find it."

"We've been trying to track it," said a tired-sounding Mystery. "It's hiding from us."

"We'll all three have to focus to search, and see if Socadan can help us," Gonamadé said. "Perhaps our combined efforts can track it down."

"I will send out my griffins to search for it from the air and to ask around if anyone has seen anything strange," Ossifer offered.

"I'll send the dragons to help," Vatron added.

"What can the rest of us do to help you?" Lask asked of Gonamadé.

"Not much I'm afraid," replied the Gateway.

"What about the Terwinus?" Lask inquired. "Androla. Is she still here? Do you suppose she could help you find Lothanvar? Surely the Merrus and the Mirror are staying together, as they are stronger that way."

"Perhaps," came a disembodied voice.

Everyone started as Androla materialized in the

midst of them where she'd been eavesdropping.

"I can attempt to seek out Lothanvar. While he is a wicked one, if he is not hiding too well, I may be able to find him, one Spirit to another."

"We would be grateful," Lask replied.

The Spirit nodded.

"Ah zaw you bring a fairy wizh you," said Asmodeus. "Zutoniuz?"

"Yes," Lask answered. "While we do not know exactly what happened yet, Fiora believes Julius did it to stop him from raising a mutiny. Salìt says he will live."

"Zhough never fly wizh ze ztate of zhoze wingz," Asmodeus said, saddened.

Lask nodded.

"Will we be giving him sanctuary?" asked Airda. "After all, he did leave with the rest of them."

"He will be safe with us, if he wishes it," Lask replied. "I imagine Julius had to coerce him quite strongly into leaving."

Chapter Forty-Six

Julius wandered his camp that evening, seeming in a rage, but lost in his heart. His soldiers recoiled from him and the rows fell into a hush when he passed. No one spoke a word to him. It was deathly quiet and Julius thought he might go mad in the silence. His feet took him to the perimeter and beyond, walking in slow steps out across the dust. There were drag marks in the dirt, smears of faintly iridescent blood, small shriveling fragments of orange wings.

"What have I done to you?" he whispered to the blood in the dust. "My brother, I have slain you. It's so quiet without you."

There were more pieces of wing and Julius felt sick at the sight. As the sun was sinking, he came to a place in the dirt where the blood had pooled, though long since soaked in. He stood over the place, surrounded by the shimmering dust and mangled pieces of wing, clenching his jaw tight at the sight. It was only then that he realized Sutonius was not laying there.

He turned, as if startled, and looked in all directions, but could not see the shape of his friend.

"Who has taken you?" he demanded of the empty desert. Looking back down, he then noticed the two sets of tracks around the place where Sutonius had lain. They were heavy tracks, and broader than the average fairy's foot; human tracks. Julius's brow furrowed and he studied them closer, noticing the slightly larger set had an imprint where the person had knelt, a faint impression behind it, a scrape in the dust. At first Julius thought it was the mark from a tail, but then it dawn on him—it was a mark from the tip of a scabbard, worn strapped across the man's back, one from a large and heavy sword.

He snarled at the ground as if it were his adversary's face, then turned, storming back across the desert, past the camp and toward the Hydra fortress. Before he could get there, he spotted the dark blue hydra Aldebaran coming toward him, looking to be in a hurry.

"Fairy!" the hydra snapped. "King Cazour has summoned you."

"I imagine I already know why," Julius growled, opening his wings and flitting past the hydra and over the wall of the stronghold.

When he reached the throneroom, Cazour roared at

him,

"Julius! One of your fairies has taken my prisoner!"

"They have not," Julius retorted. "I haven't sent anyone near here."

"My hydras saw a green winged fairy in the castle today. He said he was *your* interrogator!"

"A lie," snarled Julius. "My second, who I had thrown out into the desert, was taken also. There were human tracks around him—"

"But there was a fairy—"

"A trick. The United are allied with the Ancients, no doubt they used their magic to deceive you. It was Lask who was here, I am certain of it."

"And none of your fairies saw anything?"

"No."

"This is an outrage! The United dare to come into my lands? The Somadar dares to set foot in my castle unannounced?"

"That is precisely the audacity that caused me to leave him," Julius replied. "And they have taken Sutonius—"

"Why does that matter? I have lost a most valuable prisoner, where you have only lost some mutineer's body—"

"I cannot even give him the proper rites now!" Julius shot back. "I counted him as my brother—"

"Yet you were the one who killed him."

"Because *you* forced me to!"

"I forced you into nothing, fairy." Cazour gave an amused chuckle. "Don't tell me you regret it? Surely you are not that soft?"

Julius turned his back on the hydra and stormed out of the throneroom. Cazour just shook his heads and laughed.

Chapter Forty-Seven

The dreams were fruitless. Far and wide, Ari called the name Falsanthur, imagined the dragon appearing to her, but he was nowhere to be found. She was beginning to think he too, had perished, when one night, an old man wandered into her dream.

She stood on the edge of a sea, the water crashing just beyond her feet, when he approached her. Ari regarded him, wary, for she did not know him. He came to stand next to her, silent, looking out at the horizon. He was tall, and dignified for his age, standing with no sign of stooping or pain. His silver hair was thick and wavy, combed back from his weathered face. He had a large, stately nose, and bright blue eyes. He leaned—more for show than necessity it seemed—on a plain black wood cane.

"Nice day," he remarked.

"I suppose it is," Ari replied.

"What's a girl like you doing out here?"

"I could ask why an old fellow like you is here, too."

"Ah, but I asked first." There was a twinkle in his blue eyes.

"I'm looking for someone."

"Yes, I thought that was you shouting," said the old man. "Who was it you were calling for?"

"Falsanthur."

"Oh, it's been many years since I have heard that name." He seemed pleased by the sound of it.

"You knew him?"

"Oh, yes. I knew him very well."

"Did you meet him when he was on Earth?"

"I suppose you could say that." The old man turned to look at her. "Who might you be? Why is a pretty young girl like you looking for some old forgotten dragon?"

"I am Ariana Somadàrsath," she replied. "I am looking for the dragons left on Earth for a friend, another dragon."

"Oh? Who?"

"Scoarin. She was just recently flung to some where and when on Earth by the Mirror of Dùmsaro. I promised her I would seek out any dragons left on Earth so that she would not have to be alone."

"And have you found any?"

"Just one, named Ajikhan."

The old man hummed, nodding a bit.

"Who are you?" Ari asked, wondering what this old man was doing in her dream. "Do you know anything about Falsanthur, or what has become of him?"

"Yes, I know those things very well," he answered. "He still lives, though not as well as he once did." He extended a hand to her. "Pleased to meet you Ariana, of Lu`corian's line. There was a time I was called Falsanthur."

Ari paused in shaking his hand, brow furrowed.

"That's impossible," she said. "Falsanthur was a dragon."

"As I was," the old man replied. He saw how perplexed she was, so looked back out to sea, and told her, "I was lucky enough to be cast back to Earth before so much had moved on. I thought about finding the Gate to go back, for I feared for the egg I had left behind—poor dear, I had brought it from Earth, you know, after its mother was killed. It was all I had left of a family. However, I did not know when I had been sent to, and for all I knew my egg was dead or hatched, or had already lived a long life and died. I decided since I had made it to Etheria only to be sent back again, I was not meant to be there. I traveled, carefully of course, for there were many knights who would have liked to mount my teeth on their shields. In time, a man came to me, a great man of magic. He had need of some dragon blood for a bit of magic he was working, and I told him I would give it freely if he could help me.

I told him of my plight, and how I feared I could have no safe place on Earth, and he quite agreed with me. There was no place for dragons in the world, not live ones anyway. He told me he was a great master of transfiguration, that he could turn people into birds or fish, or most anything they wanted. He told me he could change me into something else too. I told him I wanted a form I could be safe in, where I would not be hunted, where I could live well and be respected. So, he made me into this. He went on to do some magic for a king and I never saw him again. I have lived many centuries in this form, travelling from place to place. I can't stay anywhere more than a decade or so, for then people start to realize this old man doesn't seem to get much older. I may not be immortal, but dragons have very long lives."

Ari marveled at him, almost disbelieving.

"Where is your friend Scoarin bound? Where is this Ajikhan? Perhaps I will visit him also."

Ari told him the way Ajikhan had described.

"Somewhere in the east then," mused Falsanthur, "Yes. That would be lovely. I have long thought of making passage to India. I daresay it might be time. Perhaps from there, I will find the last of our kind in this world."

Chapter Forty-Eight

Lask returned to the healer's tent that night. Sutonius lay wheezing in the flickering candlelight, pallid and hollow looking. Salìt had bandaged his back as best he could around the wings, once proud graceful wings which now hung limp, down on either side of the bed, seeming faded and without shine. Lask sat down beside him, leaning against one of the supporting poles of the tent, looking at the fairy he had come to call a friend, who was now a man in ruins. Lask did not want to think of the pain that would await him when he woke.

Lask stayed in the healer's tent that night, and did not even realize he had fallen asleep until he awoke to the faint light of dawn filtering through the canvas. He looked down to see Myranda asleep beside him, her head resting on his leg. He tried to shift free without waking her so he could get up, but was not successful. She stirred at his motion.

"Sorry," he whispered.

"You could have told me you planned to stay here," she answered. "I finally decided to go looking for you about midnight."

"Sorry," he whispered again. "I thought I had."

She patted his leg with a forgiving hand and sat up, stretching. She looked to where Sutonius lay, still asleep.

"His color's a bit better this morning," she noted.

Lask nodded, glad to see that Sutonius no longer had the pallor of a dead man. Myranda stood up, slipping out to go get dressed. Lask rose after a moment, about to do the same, when he noticed Sutonius's head move, his hazel eyes blinking in the dim light.

"Where am I?" he whispered, voice hoarse.

"In the United's camp," Lask replied, going to his side.

"I'm not dead," said the fairy, sounding disappointed.

"No. We found you in time and Salìt did what he could."

Sutonius planted his hands against the bed, pushing himself up with a grunt. Lask was going to protest, but the fairy was already getting up, so Lask took his arm to steady him. Sutonius stretched with a pained growl.

"Julius's work," he murmured. "Forgive me. I should have been stronger sooner, before he forced us to leave."

"It is not your fault," Lask replied. He tried to guide the fairy back down, saying, "You shouldn't be up yet. You need to rest so you can heal."

Sutonius stood fast, looking off to the side, with a stricken face. Lask followed his gaze to see the fairy had caught sight of himself in the mirror in the corner. He batted Lask's arm off of him and limped over on unsteady legs, going to stand before his reflection. He reached out, touching trembling fingers to the cold glass, tracing them over the ragged lines of unfamiliar wings. He reached back, finding the same battered edges behind him. He looked at himself, hardly knowing the man in the mirror.

Lask stood behind him, not knowing what to say, feeling sick at the sheer horrified agony that played over Sutonius's face. The fairy turned away from the mirror, unable to look at himself, and started to crumple into the corner. Lask went to help him, but Sutonius smacked his hands away, sinking down into the corner, drawing his knees up to his chest and bowing his head down against them. A tear glistened at the corner of his eye, slipping away down his cheek. Lask stood by, helpless and aching at the sight.

"Go," Sutonius whispered.

Lask didn't want to leave him, not like this.

"Just go," came the fairy's whisper.

Lost, and not knowing what else to do, Lask obeyed,

slipping out of the tent to leave the fairy alone with his sorrow.

Chapter Forty-Nine

The Ancients and Socadan were seated in a circle outside of the camp, heads bowed, still and silent. As the sun sank low, Lask sent several soldiers to stand guard around them, knowing they would work through the night if need be to find the Mirror. The griffins and the dragons came back with negative reports, flying out again after only a brief rest, expanding their searches further. Lask himself stood on the perimeter under the flapping banner in the gathering darkness, knowing nothing else to do but wait.

The next morning, Lask spotted Sutonius sitting outside the healer's tent in the sunlight, taking a breath of fresh air. His tragic wings still fanned instinctually in the light, casting pulsating shadows over his scabbed back. Lask noticed that people seemed to be avoiding him, not knowing what to say in such a situation and giving him a wide berth to avoid having to enter into such an awkward conversation. Lask, however, came to fold his long legs to settle onto the bench beside him. Sutonius looked over at him with drowned eyes.

"I wanted to tell you yesterday, but I thought it would not be a very good time," Lask said. "The council agrees you still have a place here among us."

"I am an outcast," said Sutonius. "My people are now traitors and I cannot return to them. They likely all think I'm dead anyway. I betrayed all of you with my silence, so I do not truly belong here anymore either."

"I imagine Julius did everything he could to force you into it."

"That is no excuse."

"You do not need an excuse," Lask replied. "I know you and I know you are a good man. All of the others know that too. So long as that continues to be the case, you are welcome among us. We cannot hold you culpable for your general's folly."

Sutonius shook his head, running a hand through his tangled auburn hair.

"You pity me," he said.

"I am saddened that this has happened to someone I respect and care about," Lask replied. "If that is pity, then yes. You have lost far more than what could ever be deserved and I would not place another wrong on you by casting you out or treating you with anything less than compassion."

Sutonius looked over at him, and Lask could tell he was trying to decide whether to speak or not.

"I feel so very lost," he confessed, and looked away again. "I do not know what to do. My best friend has destroyed my life, and I do not know why. I cannot go home, perhaps not ever. Everything I was, everything I knew and thought, has been changed forever."

Lask watched him, feeling the sheer gravity of Sutonius's situation pulling at him. After a moment, he said,

"Perhaps not *everything*. We are still your friends, and you still belong with us. We are all a bunch of misfits in our own way, I suppose. The Unicorns walked out on us during the fight against Vortearigan. The griffins had a rogue that led a war on the kingdom. The centaurs are all half mad, and apparently I had an Ancient in my head for half my life and didn't even know it. I should think a displaced fairy would fit right in."

Sutonius gave a slight smile.

"True, I suppose," he conceded.

Chapter Fifty

That evening, Chai Karan and the Gateway approached Lask after dinner. Seeing them, Lask asked immediately,

"Have you found Lothanvar?"

"We have not," the drokamerdor replied. "He and the Mirror hide from our magic well. We are but taking a rest and will return to our search later tonight. In the meantime, I am prepared to capture Lothanvar's memory; however, I require your assistance."

"Of course," Lask replied, rising to follow them through the camp. On a small table, there was a seemingly innocuous hand mirror. Chai Karan motioned for Lask to pick it up.

"I have enchanted this mirror to capture the images of whatever is reflected in it. To activate it, it will need to be wetted with blood. As there is great magic in your blood, I believe having you be the one to activate it will make the magic all the more effective. I will tell you when to do so."

"How are we going to capture the Spirit's memory if he is no longer here?" Lask inquired.

"I will take us back in time to the night he committed the crime."

"You'll probably regret having just eaten dinner," Gonamadé remarked.

Lask glanced over at him, wary, then tucked the mirror under his arm and stepped forward to place a hand on Chai Karan's furry shoulder. He felt the Ancient's magic prickle over him and everything lurched, as when he had traveled with Gonamadé, but this time the scenery whipped past them, blurred images flying by like raindrops, too fast to see, and all of a sudden they came to an abrupt halt. Lask staggered and caught himself on Chai Karan, feeling dizzy.

"It will pass," Chai Karan said, unconcerned.

Lask shook his head as if to clear it.

They were in Farisdon, albeit a much smaller version of the city. Lask guessed it could not have been more than a few centuries after the city was first built. It was nighttime, and there were only a few people on the streets.

"Can't they see us?" Lask asked.

"No," Time replied. "As neither of us were here at

this moment in time, we are but observers. No one will see or hear us. I could make myself known if I wished, as I am Time, but we will need this stealth tonight. Come. It will be soon."

Lask followed the drokamerdor away down the street. Chai Karan walked in a straight line, and anyone in his way passed through him like a ghost. Lask was less willing to walk through people, and so wove his way around them in the Ancient's wake. Chai Karan led him out of the city and Lask was curious.

"What are we looking for?" he asked.

"Lothanvar will do a terrible thing this night. We must be at his home when he arrives to do it."

The Ancient made his way to a house outside the city. It was a modest place, though Lask could tell from the elegant ironwork hinges and the panes of colored glass in a few of the windows that the residents were in no want of money. Chai Karan walked straight through the front door and Lask followed, feeling a chill pass over him as he walked through into the foyer.

It was a well-furnished place, with subtle hints of finery; mahogany furniture, bits of gold on the decorations, a tapestry on the far wall. Chai Karan took no interest in the place, following the main hall through the house to the backmost room, passing into the kitchen. Lask followed him, seeing a table at the side of the room, where an uneaten supper was in the process of being cleared away. The candles on the table had burned low, and by their flickering light, Lask watched the woman taking up the plate she had eaten on, having given up on waiting for whomever was supposed to sit opposite her. There was a paper in the center of the table; a contract of marriage, Lask recognized.

She was many months pregnant, likely to give birth in only a few weeks. She patted a hand on her belly as she carried the plate over to wash it in the basin on the counter and told the baby not to be so excitable. Lask studied her face, suddenly realizing why she seemed familiar.

"That's Androla!" he exclaimed.

"Yes," said Chai Karan, indifferent to the fact.

Lask suddenly realized exactly what was going to happen, and about that time, there was the sound of glass breaking outside. Androla stood up on tiptoe, peering out the window into the darkness, a look of concern furrowing over her face.

Lothanvar came barging in through the back door. He was just as burly as his Merrus form, with cold grey eyes and dark tangled hair.

"Lothanvar," said Androla, trying to sound pleased to see him, but Lask could hear the fear under her voice.

He stumbled into the kitchen, saying,

"*You*. You and that *rat* in your belly."

"You're drunk," Androla said, backing away from him. "You stink of cheap ale."

"If you weren't so stingy with that fortune of yours, I could have gotten wine," he answered.

"Activate the mirror," Chai Karan told Lask.

Lask obeyed, pricking his finger on the tip of his knife and smearing a line of blood across the surface of the mirror. It shone with the light of magic and Lask angled it toward the pair in the kitchen.

"You keep me poor," Lothanvar was saying. "What's the use of a rich wife if you can't even get a good drink from marrying her?"

"I signed the breaking line today," Androla growled.

"What was that?" asked Lothanvar, inclining his head toward her.

"I was going to try to talk to you one last time over dinner. You said you'd be here. You didn't show, so I signed it." She pointed to the table, where their marriage contract lay, with her signature on the breaking line, rendering it void.

"You wench," snarled Lothanvar. "What am I supposed to do? You own every damn thing in the house."

"That's not my concern anymore," Androla told him.

Lothanvar lunged at her, grabbing her by the arm.

"Get off me!" she snapped, struggling.

"You think you can just leave?" Lothanvar spat at her.

"You think you can just walk out on *me?*"

"Let go," yelped Androla, pulling against him, and the fear began to break through her mask of resolve.

"Chai Karan," Lask growled. It was all he could do to stand by and watch Androla be abused.

"It's already happened," the Ancient replied. "There's nothing we can do."

"You're not going anywhere," Lothanvar roared. "I'll chain you up if I have to. Maybe then I can get that key to your moneybox—"

"Stop it! You're hurting me. The baby—"

"I never wanted a whelp!" Lothanvar growled. "It's your own damn fault for not knowing when you were in season."

"We can talk about this when you're sober. You can stay here. I'll go spend the night in the inn—"

"You're not going *anywhere*!" Lothanvar roared again.

Androla clawed at his face with her nails and broke free of him. Lothanvar howled and went after her, grabbing her by the hair and yanking her backwards. Lask saw his other hand reaching, stretching for the counter. He stepped forward on instinct, but found Chai Karan's wing holding him back. Lothanvar's hand closed around the knife there as he roared,

"I'll stake you to the floor! See if you can leave me then!"

Androla screamed as the knife pierced into her shoulder. She struggled, pulling against him, but Lothanvar tackled her over onto the floor and drove the knife into her chest, drawing another scream from her. Androla writhed under him, screaming and crying, and Lask looked on, horrified, held back by Chai Karan's wing and the tail that had coiled around his ankle.

Lothanvar held her to the floor, thick arm falling into a rhythm, stabbing her again and again until she stopped screaming, the life of her and their child pooled beneath her. Lothanvar sat back, wiping the splattered blood off his face. Lask looked on, disgusted and enraged, disturbed in every possible way.

"Come," said Chai Karan. "We have what we need. He will clean the place well; there is nothing more to see."

The scene faded as everything lurched again, the Ancient's magic towing them over the kingdom and through history once more, landing back where they had been in the United's camp. Gonamadé was waiting for them.

"Did you get it?" he asked, eager.

Lask passed the mirror to him, silent, and walked away from the two Ancients without another word. Gonamadé let him go, sensing his distress. Lask wandered back through the camp to his tent at the center and went inside. Myranda was out, so he sank into the chair in the corner, rubbing a hand over his eyes as if he could wipe away what they had seen. He sat there in the silence, though still hearing Androla's screams. The horrified look must have been lingering on his face, because when Myranda came in, she asked immediately,

"What in the world?"

"I have witnessed a murder," Lask replied.

"The memory?"

He nodded.

Myranda came over to him, but Lask stood up to meet her, drawing her into his arms.

"It was Androla," he told her. "Lothanvar's wife. She was pregnant and he murdered her. He just kept stabbing her..." Lask bowed his head into Myranda's bright hair, inhaling its familiar scent.

"There was nothing you could have done," she replied, hugging him tighter. "I know that doesn't make it any better, but it was done long ago. The only thing you can do is try to it to make things right now."

Lask nodded, holding her against him, feeling her warmth through their clothes.

"I just," he paused. "I cannot imagine how a man could do such a horrible thing to his wife. Even if he did not love her, to destroy the mother of one's child—"

"Evil needs no reason," said Myranda. "That is part of the very nature of evil. It is useless to worry over how and why, when there is no answer to be had. Reason is very often what separates the good from the wicked." She looked up at him and took his face in her hand. "And it is what drives the good so mad when he sees wickedness."

Chapter Fifty-One

Ossifer's padded feet were silent as he crept through the trees. Morpheus was behind him, equally quiet. They crouched low over the grass, wings tucked down tight, ears flattened back. They had spied the pair of hydras from the air, making their way through the western edges of Correneth. The griffins had landed in the woods, stalking the hydras, trying to discern their purpose. Ossifer opened one wing to stop his son as one of the hydras stopped.

"That's it, Selat, I've had enough," the hydra announced. He flopped out on the grass. "We've been running all day."

"We can't stop!" said the one called Selat. "We've got to make it to the High Peaks by the day after tomorrow. We'll never make it in time if you keep stopping."

The other hydra snorted, and wrapped his tail around himself, making no move to get up.

"Mìtov!" snapped Selat.

"An hour's rest won't kill you," Mìtov answered. "Besides, look at this grass. It's awfully comfortable."

"Ack, foul greenery—"

"It's better than the hard dust we usually have to sleep on."

Selat growled, but nonetheless settled down in the grass under the trees to rest. Ossifer and Morpheus crept in closer, hiding themselves behind a thick curtain of brush off to one side.

"You'd best not let that running mouth of yours get us in trouble," grumbled Selat. "If you let on that we've been stopping as much as we have—"

"No one's going to know but you. I don't even see why we're going all the way up there. Syringa saw a lake. Could've been any number of lakes."

"There's only one lake amid mountains with a city on the shore."

"Could've been in the Arayans. Those drokamerdors have their castle on a mountain lake."

"We don't get to decide where to go."

"That's for sure—"

"And you'd better be careful grousing like that. If Aldebaran were to hear your insolence, you'd be no better off than poor Sergar was."

Mìtov shuddered.

"Although," Mìtov remarked, pushing the unpleasant memory aside, "If the United can't control it, I don't know what Cazour's planning to do with it."

"*If* he can get it," muttered Selat. "If that old fortune teller Syringa can find it, you know the Ancients will know where it is. They're probably already there."

"I hope not. Cazour's going to make his war against the kingdom any time now. If we can't get the Mirror, we're not going to have a chance, but that won't stop Cazour from attacking. We'll be dead for sure."

"I doubt that. We've still got a good three thousand who are in fighting shape—"

"And the United number close to twelve thousand."

"Under ten thousand now, I'd wager, with the Fairies gone from them."

Mìtov gave a derisive snort.

"Fairies," he said, "A lot of help those puny wretches will be."

Selat didn't argue. The two fell into a brooding silence, and it wasn't long before a deep rumbling reverberated through the darkness. Ossifer realized Mìtov had drifted off to sleep, snoring. Selat remained awake, though two of his heads had their eyes closed. The dominant head looked drowsy, but he kept the other two heads alert, keeping watch around them. One glanced toward the brush and the head cocked slightly, eyes narrowing.

The other heads perked up, curious, turning toward the brush as well.

Ossifer and Morpheus hunkered lower, their black feathers blending into the shadows. Neither dared to breathe as Selat's dominant head snaked over, mouth opening in a slight hiss. Mìtov snorted, awakened by the sound.

"What?" he grumbled. He followed his companion's gaze, looking confused. "Are those…?"

"Eyes," Selat finished.

"Fly, Morpheus!" squawked Ossifer.

The two griffins leapt into the air as the hydra lunged for their hiding place, jaws snapping through the brambles, and they could feel the rush of wind as three sets of teeth snapped closed right behind them. The pair flung themselves into the air, up through the trees, disappearing in the black sky.

Chapter Fifty-Two

Lask slept little that night, unable to shake the image of Androla's murder. When he rose in the morning, he went out to get water from the barrel nearby, bringing a handful up to splash over his face. When he looked up, he started, finding Androla standing there across from him. She recognized the look in his face, and said,

"I suppose you were successful in collecting Lothanvar's memory, then?"

"Yes," Lask replied. "Why did you not tell us?"

"I do not like to remember that night. While I would likely be at peace had it been only me that was murdered, I cannot rest knowing the murderer of my child was never known."

"He will receive what is due him," Lask promised her.

"I wonder," said Androla, "Would you permit me to be the one who shows him the memory? It would give me great satisfaction."

"I think we could arrange that."

"I found him," Androla said. "I do not think he knew I was there, so will likely remain there."

"Where?"

"He and the Mirror hide on a wrecked fishing boat on the Lake of Goltor."

Chapter Fifty-Three

Ossifer and Morpheus returned as the council was gathering.

"We know where the Mirror is," Ossifer crowed.

"As do I," Lask replied. "Androla was able to locate Lothanvar. She says he and the Mirror are hiding on the Lake of Goltor. Does that agree with the information you found?"

"It does," said Ossifer, "Although we have a bit of a problem. The Hydras' seer, Syringa, found the Mirror too. They're on their way to the north as we speak."

"Can the Ancients take us there?" Lask asked of Gonamadé who was sitting in on the meeting.

"Perhaps. It would take some time though if we were going to have to move any large number."

"The hydras said they were to be at the lake by tomorrow," Ossifer replied, "And from the sounds of it, there will be quite a lot of them gathering there."

"Then we should take a fair number of our soldiers," Lask replied, "To help defend Farisdon and keep them at bay while we finish the Mirror."

"To magically move an army," said the Gateway, "Can't be done. Leastways not in the time constraints. It would be an exhausting task and we can only take at most maybe twenty or thirty humans in one go. To move *thousands,* many much larger creatures, and with only three Ancients—"

"Then we'd better set out with all haste," Lask finished.

Chapter Fifty-Four

"What have you seen?" hissed the Mirror when the dark shape of Lothanvar floated back into the wreck.

"Hydras," hissed the Spirit. "Coming northward, looking for us. If they know where we are, then the United surely do as well. We should move on before they find us here."

"And are we to flee from them forever?" Maléchian inquired. "We have proven before that our power can challenge the Ancients'—"

"They will surely cast me into Hell—"

"When they open the Gate to do so, we could throw them in instead."

Lothanvar's white eyes glinted as they turned, intrigued, back to the Mirror.

"Think of it," Maléchian hissed, "With the Ancients cast out, there would be no power left in this world that could challenge us. We would make quick work of the United and the nobility who rule this kingdom. It could be ours, to sow with all the chaos and evil we could feast on. Besides, the only way they could permanently cast you to Hell is if they properly condemn you, and the only way they could do *that* is if they talked to that wretched wife of yours, who's been long dead these past millennia."

"How right you are, my friend," rumbled Lothanvar. "Yes, if they cannot condemn me, they cannot break you, and as long as we have one another to draw power from we are a force to be reckoned with indeed." The Merrus seemed to swell with dark resolve. "Yes, let us await these Ancients and rid ourselves of them once and for all."

Chapter Fifty-Five

The United were on the move by mid-afternoon. Lask sent the dragons and griffins out ahead of them to track the hydras and to send an advance warning to Farisdon.

"Deliver the message yourself," Lask told Ossifer, "And go into the city alone. Tell the Estara to prepare the city for any attack the hydras might make, but have her do so quietly. Let no public announcement of our coming be made. We cannot afford to scare the Mirror away and start our search over again."

Ossifer nodded and soared out over the rolling hills beyond, toward the distant spires deepening twilight and into the night, but it was not until it was very late that Lask allowed them to stop. The soldiers rested for a while, but did not make camp. The weather was fair and so the force slept in the velveteen grass under the glittering heavens.

Lask was too restless to sleep. He got up, so not to disturb Myranda with his tossing and turning, and took to wandering among his sleeping soldiers. He passed in silence under the faint low-burning torchlight, looking with all the watchful concern of a father over the creatures who rested in the cool night air. There were a few still awake, restless as he was, sitting beside small campfires, talking in low murmurs amongst themselves. They nodded to their commander, making the motions of sleepy salutes as he passed. Lask spotted a pair of folded gold wings and went to sit down by the fire across from the Gateway.

"Too fretted to sleep," Gonamadé remarked. It was not a question, as Lask was sure the Ancient could feel the thoughts stirring about his mind.

Lask nodded. Noticing the fire was burning low, he took up a stick to rearrange a few of the logs, only to have Gonamadé point a finger at them and make them roar back to life. Lask drew back, escaping with a few mildly-singed fingers.

"Sorry," mumbled the Gateway.

"What must we do tomorrow?" Lask inquired, deciding not to remark on the blaze.

"A few of us will go out to the wreck where the Merrus is hiding, Androla will show him the memory and then I must cast him through to Hell." He took a breath, looking into the flames. "The Gate to Hell is a terrible thing. You should stay far back from it when I open it."

Lask nodded. The Gateway seemed to be lost in thought and Lask could feel the nervous energy seeping over from the Ancient's mind. Sensing that Lask had picked up on it, Gonamadé got up and said,

"Well, I suppose I'll try to get some sleep to pass the time."

Lask knew the Ancient didn't even *need* to sleep, but nonetheless let him go. It wasn't long until someone came to take his place, the slender cloaked figure settling down beside him. Lask glanced over at her and Mystery scooted over closer to him until her thigh was pressed against his. Lask shifted over a bit to put a few inches between them. Mystery let out that quiet, girlish laugh.

"You're awfully happy considering what we will be facing tomorrow," Lask remarked.

"Tomorrow will be fine," Mystery replied.

"Sure of that, are you?"

"It's impossible to be *sure* of anything, but I know what is most likely going to happen, so I'm not terribly worried about it."

Lask wished he could share the Ancient's certainty.

"Will the hydras be there?" he asked.

"What will you give me if I tell you?"

Lask sighed, sorry he had bothered to ask. Mystery

smiled and hooked her arm in his, taking his hand in her own. Lask tried to shift free of her, but she had an unnaturally strong grip for such a slight frame, aided by her magic, no doubt. Mystery smiled, and stroked his knuckles with her other hand saying,

"Yes, the hydras will be there, but they will ultimately be too late. This time, anyway."

"What does that mean?"

Mystery shifted over again so their legs touched. Lask tried to evade her, but she still kept a grip on his arm and said,

"If you're going to keep asking me questions, I ought to get *something* out of it." She smiled at him from the shadows of her hood. "Be glad a little friendly cuddle is all I want."

Lask made an irritated noise, but sat still as Mystery leaned her head against his shoulder to say,

"You will need much strength in the days to come. Though the evil of the Mirror will be defeated, its evil shall spark one much greater. What has long simmered shall burst into flame, and thus burning, shall burn many things."

"What are you talking about?"

"You will need to seek one in Advasad, on the Shores of Fangàn. He can help you when the Hydras make their move." She twined her fingers in his. "And look for one among your enemies, one as blue as the velveteen night, with eyes of sorrow."

"I don't understand."

Mystery tilted her head up, brushing back his hair, to whisper in his ear,

"You are a tempest of fire, Lask, and though that flame shall light the world, one night it will get the better of you and burn the wayward subjects of your fury. There shall be much sadness then, but do not let your pride keep that fire burning."

Lask turned his head to look at her, finding her face mere inches from his. He studied her, not knowing what she meant, but hearing the gravity in her voice, and seeing the sadness in her eyes in the flickering firelight. He shifted free of her, and she released him. Though he did not understand the Ancient's words, they nonetheless unnerved him, and he left her by the fire, slipping back into the darkness to the place where Myranda slept. Lask settled down beside her, quiet so not to wake her, but Myranda's voice came through the shadows.

"What did she want?"

"Who?"

"The Ancient you were getting cozy with by the fire."

Lask turned onto his side, snuggling up against the back of her to put an arm around her.

"She was telling me some things. She would only tell

me if I let her sit close to me."

"And what did she have to say?"

"Nothing I particularly understood," Lask replied. "Though I expect it will make sense when the time comes." He kissed her shoulder.

"I don't like her being that close to you."

"I think she's harmless."

"Just because I wasn't supposed to see it doesn't make it any better."

"Surely you're not worried, darling. You must know me better than that."

"It's not *you* I'm worried about." Myranda turned her head back to kiss him. "She bewitched you once; she could do it again and I might not be there to barge in next time."

Lask put his head on her shoulder. Before he could answer, Myranda remarked,

"These Ancients, they're such trouble. It's bad enough Gonamadé's seen me naked."

"And then some."

Myranda reached back to smack at him, but Lask could hear her laughing through the darkness.

Chapter Fifty-Six

Ari tried not to intrude on Scoarin, for she thought her presence only reminded the dragon of all that was lost to her. Nonetheless, she could not help but seek her to find out how she fared. It had been weeks since last she found the dragon, but Scoarin appeared when Ari called, and she looked a bit brighter than she had before.

"Ari," said Scoarin with a nod.

"How are you?" asked Ari. "Where are you?"

"I reached mountains three days ago. I have found Ajikhan. He is gruff and out of practice with dealing with others, but he is kind enough, and I think he will grow friendlier with time. His cave is spacious and well hidden. He says I can stay as long as I like, forever if it pleases me. I think he is glad to have a friend again, and I think we will be safe here."

"That is very good," said Ari. "I have news of

Falsanthur."

"Yes? Does he live?"

"He does. He is very well, although..." Ari paused, not sure how to explain. "He is not a dragon anymore."

"What do you mean, child?" Scoarin tilted her head, confused.

"He said he met a wizard long ago, and the wizard changed him into a man. Falsanthur has lived as a human for centuries."

Scoarin rumbled, taking this in. At length, she said,

"I suppose that is the only reason he is still alive."

"He said he would make his way to where you are. That is, if you are there in the years when he arrives."

"I would be pleased to see him," said Scoarin, "And I imagine Ajikhan would be too, even if Falsanthur should appear as a man." She thought this over and nodded. "Yes. It may be that he could help us a great deal, for he could travel freely, learn, and acquire things that we could not. He could be a great ally if he should join us here."

"I suspect he will," Ari told her.

"You have likely saved what is left of my life, Ariana," said Scoarin. "And though I have no way to ever repay you, you have my thanks. Always."

"I would never do less for you," Ari replied, "For you have always been a dear friend to my family, and we grieve your disappearance as if you were one of our own."

Scoarin managed a faint smile.

"Tell Calliban I love him," she said. "Perhaps there will be a time when my heart is strong enough to visit him in dreams. Until then, I shall live as well as I can with what I have, and be grateful I am not alone, all thanks to you."

Chapter Fifty-Seven

When dawn came, the United were already traveling again. Lask had sent Ossifer and several griffins out to look for the Hydras an hour or two before sunup, and it was still early in the morning when Ossifer came swooping back, crowing,

"The Hydras have reached Farisdon! The city has been sealed off, but they clamor at the gates. The soldiers there have begun to engage them from the walls, but their arrows can do little damage against so thick a hide."

"Vatron!" called Lask. "Take your dragons and fly to the city! Engage the Hydras as best you can. We will be close behind you."

Vatron nodded and leapt into the sky, roaring for the dragons to follow her. Lask called for a quickened pace and the United raced away over the hills toward the mountains. It was late morning when they arrived at Farisdon, and as they crested a hill within view of the city, they could see the chaos below.

There were perhaps a thousand hydras stamping and writhing outside the city, clawing at the gates, heads snapping up at the soldiers on the walls. The dragons wheeled above them in the air, dropping onto them with fire and vengeful claws, wrestling with them on the ground.

The horns sounded the charge and the United plowed into the hydras from the south, thickening the already churning chaos. Theramancer galloped, shrieking, amid the stamping feet and whipping tails, while Lask ducked the teeth snapping down at him, slicing his sword out at the thick legs crowding around them like tree trunks.

The hydras were about the same size as the dragons, but their bodies were much thicker. The moranters could hardly reach their knees to bite them, and the unicorns spent more of their time trying to avoid being stepped on while their horns glanced off of the thick skin that bound their enemies.

"Send them back!" Lask called to Forge, pointing toward the two races who were struggling amid the hydras.

The general nodded and turned his horse, calling out the orders.

The centaurs, however, were having a merry time, galloping about the battlefield, swinging their axes at the enemies' legs and tails, running up beneath them and stabbing straight up into their undersides. The griffins turned and swooped in the air, pecking at their adversaries' eyes, clawing at their necks, dodging snapping teeth.

Lask pulled back on Theramancer's reins, halting the horse's charge just long enough to avoid the crushing weight of a falling hydra as it was bowled over by one of the dragons. All of a sudden, something dropped on top of them and Theramancer screamed as he was lifted up off the ground. Lask looked to see that Vatron had grabbed them.

"You must get inside," the dragon said, "The Ancients are gathering there."

She flew up over the battlefield, carrying Lask and his kicking horse over the walls to deposit them on the other side. Theramancer bucked and shied when she set him down, and Lask patted the horse's neck, speaking into his ear to steady him. Calliban set Myranda down nearby, and bent down so Mystery could climb down from his back. Chai Karan and Gonamadé were already inside, calling,

"Come! We must get to the lake!"

Lask signaled to Ossifer, Morpheus and Marjusina in

the air and the griffins followed them from above as they rode through the city. Farisdon was teeming, soldiers running to the walls, carrying more arrows, spears, and cauldrons of boiling oil to be poured on the enemy. The citizens were shutting themselves in their homes, most trying to hide and keep out of the way, though a few ran through the streets in panic, only to be herded back by the soldiers.

The lakeshore was quieter than usual, most of the fishermen and merchants having fled back into the city proper to take shelter. Lask and Myranda left their horses on the shore and Ossifer landed for them to climb onto his back. Morpheus and Marjusina landed to carry Mystery and Socadan. They soared out over the water, leaving the clamor of the city behind. It was almost eerily quiet, a hush seeming to fall over the water.

The lake was crystalline and seemed still from high above, reflecting the mountains that encircled it and the sky in which they flew. Lask glanced skyward, seeing dark clouds rolling in from over the mountains, shrouding the sky with unnatural speed.

"They call up a storm," explained Gonamadé as he flew alongside Ossifer. "They are both weaker in the day, and so will hide from the sun however they can."

The shipwreck was on the far northwestern shore of the lake. A hulk of shattered timbers lay impaled upon the spears of rock rising out of the water. A dark mist swirled around the remains of the ship like a cloak of death itself.

"Be cautious," said Chai Karan.

They folded their wings to land down on the deck. The timbers creaked under their weight, belying their presence instantly, and they all braced for the attack they knew would come. The boat was silent, no sign of the evil that lurked within it. The Gateway stepped across the deck, slowly, carefully, a furry hand poised over his chest, ready to snatch free the key to Hell.

Lask's eyes were drawn to a faint flicker to the side and whirled to face it, but he saw only the slight outline of Androla, carrying the enchanted mirror. She brought a finger to her lips and looked down the length of the deck, pointing toward the other end of the ship. They picked their way down the deck, all tensed, ready to spring as soon as their enemy showed himself.

And show himself the Merrus did.

Lothanvar came bursting up from below in a shattering of timbers that shook the deck beneath their feet. The green light of his magic exploded in a blinding flash, and it struck the Gateway square in the chest, blasting him backward over the side of the ship.

"Ossifer, get him!" Lask shouted.

The griffin nodded and bounded over to leap off the side of the wreck.

In the flash, the Mirror appeared on deck behind them. Chai Karan swung his head back, golden magic shooting out on the sound of his roar, while Mystery unleashed her magic at Lothanvar. Socadan stood between them, arms flung wide, sending magic out at both of their enemies, looking as though he were caught in a tug-of-war between his own magic. Ossifer dropped a wet Gonamadé back onto the deck.

"Androla, the memory!" Lask called, looking for the Terwinus.

The Spirit was already there. She appeared before Lothanvar, looking more solid than ever. Her eyes blazed and her hair swirled about her head in her fury. She looked small there before him, a slender figure of pale light before the dark, writhing cloud of what was once her husband, but it was Lothanvar who recoiled.

"Too long," she roared, "Too long have you lingered in the stench of your own evil!" She slapped him across the face and Lothanvar let out a scream as her light touched him.

Behind her, the Mirror was struggling against Chai Karan and Socadan, and managed to unleash a bolt of green light at Androla, but it glanced off her, its evil unable to touch her.

"It's time for you to be given what is rightfully yours," she growled, and she thrust the mirror out for him to see, the memory of what he'd done unfolding in its surface.

Lothanvar howled and recoiled from it, but Androla reached out and grabbed him by the throat, the light of her hand hissing against his darkness and he let out a shriek, the white planes of his eyes seeming to smoke as he beheld his own crime.

Maléchian let out a roar behind them, feeling the breaking of his maker, but Chai Karan, Mystery and Socadan held the Mirror fast. The Gateway reached up to his bandolier and pulled free the lowest key of dark iron and raised it skyward, declaring,

"For this, Lothanvar, you are condemned, and as is my power here, you are now cast to your rightful place!"

Gonamadé brought the key down and pointed it straight toward the ground.

There was a high unholy shriek and a flash of fiery red light, and a hole seemed to open in the darkness around the ship. A deep resounding boom echoed over the ship and across the water, rippling out over the world, the force of it plowing over everyone in its path. Chai Karan, Mystery, Socadan, and all of the others were blasted back from it; only the Gateway stood straight before it. The open Gate was a swirling portal of fire and screams, the heat of it radiating outward, making the air shimmer and ripple. A more terrible thing Lask had never beheld.

In that gaping hole of fire there seemed to be every fear and wrong conceivable, and though he could hardly look upon it, he could feel the evil of it washing over him with the heat.

Gonamadé planted his feet, his golden magic whipping out, coiling around Lothanvar, and with a final roar, the Merrus was cast out of Etheria and through the waiting Gate into Hell. The Gateway raised the key and Lask heard him scream. The Gate to Hell snapped shut with a clap like thunder, the flash of the Gateway's golden light overpowering the fire, and in that instant, Gonamadé was gone.

Lask suddenly felt something in him snap taut and a wave of unspeakable horror swept through him, a torturous pain rushing with it. Myranda was startled when he suddenly let out a roar of agony from beside her, his fingers clawing at the deck, pulling up splinters.

"Lask!" she exclaimed, "What—?"

There was a flash of green light, accompanied by a shriek from the Mirror. In the chaos, the Ancients had been knocked from their feet and their magic severed. The Mirror's power grabbed hold of them in the moment of confusion, pinning them down to the deck.

"Break it!" screamed Mystery. "You have to break it now!"

Ossifer and Morpheus both leapt for it, only to stop

in mid-bound, running head first into a wall of green magic. Socadan was running for it as well, only to have a cord of magic coil around his ankle, yanking him to a halt and spitting the sparks of his magic back in his face. Myranda knelt on the deck, torn between making a charge for the Mirror and staying near Lask, who could hardly breathe from whatever force had a hold on him.

Lask grit his teeth, hardly able to move from the sheer agony that radiated through him, when all of a sudden, it was as if the storm calmed.

I'm still here, came the voice of the Gateway in his mind.

The pain released and the terrible stretching in his mind seemed to stop.

I'm coming back. Go!

Lask didn't waste a moment. He rolled to his feet, drawing Myranda with him, and took off down the deck toward the Mirror. Lask's sword deflected the first beam of magic, but he wasn't quick enough to catch the second that flashed out low, catching around his legs and jerking taut, stopping his charge in an instant. Myranda made it only a bit further before she too was caught in the web of green magic that Maléchian had laced around the Mirror.

Socadan forced a hand up against its power and unleashed a bolt of gold light. Maléchian snarled when it hit, and Lask felt the magic lessen just a bit, but not enough for him to break free of it.

They strained against the hold of the magic, each forcing themselves forward by one gradual step at a time, but they were a long way from the Mirror's surface. Lask sought the Gateway with his mind, but could hardly focus enough to find him while his attention was so drawn by the Mirror. He caught a glimpse of something in the sky, and thought it was Gonamadé returning.

But it wasn't. It was a bright, brave, streak of silver plummeting out of the sky. She had been smart; Marjusina had leapt overboard as soon as the power of the Gate let go, and she had since circled high and unseen into the sky, out of sight of the Mirror. She came diving back now, wings tucked in tight against her sides, sending her free falling out of the heavens, the light of the magic glinting off her feathers, making her glow like a silver comet. The griffin plunged straight down at the deck before Maléchian could catch her, flaring her wings at the last second. Her claws dug in, screeching her to a halt as they pulled deep furrows into the face of the Mirror.

Maléchian screamed and in the moment of surprise and pain, his magic snapped, and his adversaries' charge resumed with all the pent up might that had been held back in them. The Ancients' magic shot forward in the same instant that Lask's sword pommel and Myranda's spear pole came pounding down onto the Mirror's surface just as Marjusina bashed her fist between

Maléchian's eyes.

The Mirror's surface shattered into a thousand pieces, and Maléchian's scream dissipated among the sound of them clattering down. A roll of thunder exploded as the Mirror's power was broken, and the dark clouds and mist that had gathered were swept away, the bright radiance of the sun bursting back down upon them with all its light and promise.

They stood over the shards of the Mirror, looking down upon them, and from behind them came Chai Karan's rumble of,

"Well done."

Lask looked over his shoulder to see the drokamerdor wore a rare look of satisfaction. Mystery smiled at him from under her hood. Socadan just snorted, *hrmph,* and nodded.

The griffins picked them up and deposited them on the lakeshore beyond the wreck. Chai Karan landed beside Mystery, and the two nodded at each other in unspoken agreement. Mystery raised her hands, golden light swirling out from them, and the magic hit the front of the wreck, wrenching it free of the rocks, and shoving it back out into the water. Once free, it bubbled and rocked, sinking at last below the surface, carrying the now useless frame of the Mirror deep to the bottom of the crystalline lake.

There was a flicker off to the side and they looked to see Androla there.

"Thank you," said the Spirit, "I am now free to have the peace I have long desired."

She opened her arms as if to embrace the world, closing her eyes and tilting her head back with a look of profound peace and satisfaction. Her form glowed brighter and brighter until she dissolved into her own light, passing on to whatever glory had long awaited her.

The companions were silent for a moment in the wake of her passing.

"It's finally over," said Socadan, having lived to witness both the Mirror's creation and its destruction.

"And now," Lask said to the Ancients, "I imagine there are some guards at Farisdon who would most welcome your help with the Hydras."

Chapter Fifty-Eight

Chai Karan landed on the ramparts of Farisdon, roaring out over the melee, his magic thundering out over the scene. Below, the Hydra force was battered, having been harried by the dragons and the twirling spears of the centaurs and human soldiers. At the sight of the Ancients on the battlements and their swirling magic, many of the hydras turned and fled the field, knowing that the Mirror, the object of their fight, must now surely be lost to them.

"Stand!" came a voice above the chaos. "Cowards!"

Lask looked down from the ramparts to see a dark blue hydra roaring at his fellows, the one he knew was called Aldebaran. He watched as the hydra's companions left him, fleeing one by one from the wrath of the dragons and the Ancients, the fight having left them entirely. Aldebaran stood fast for a moment, finding himself alone among the blood and the fallen forms of his fellows. The hydra's eyes turned back toward Farisdon, finding Lask on the battlements, and for a moment their eyes held.

The hydra's gaze was not one of rage, but the resigned sorrow of defeat, a reluctance for bloodshed, the fear of one who must deliver failure back to his king. As he looked down upon the hydra who now stood alone, Lask felt a pang of pity and the words of Mystery suddenly rang in his mind: *look for one among your enemies, one as blue as the velveteen night, with eyes of sorrow.*

Vatron landed beside the hydra, roaring in his faces, flaring her wings, but Aldebaran did not engage her. His eyes broke from Lask's and he turned, galloping away over the carnage after his fellows, and as he ran, Lask knew he and the hydra would likely see much more of each other in the coming days.

A cheer went up from the soldiers below, rising up, joining with the cheer from those on the ramparts. Lask stood silent, looking southward after the hydras who had fled, and he knew that their victory on this day would not last.

Chapter Fifty-Nine

They stayed in the city of Farisdon that night, and as they made their way along the streets, Lask walked hand in hand with Myranda. Marjusina walked beside him as well and he said to her,

"We all owe you a great measure of thanks."

"An honor to be of assistance," the griffin replied with a smile. "I hope, perhaps, I might continue to be of close assistance to you in the future, sir. Though I have not much ambition, I find being around you to be most exciting."

Lask chuckled at the griffin's grin.

"I am always in need of a good friend," he replied. He put an arm around the griffin's feathery neck as they walked the streets toward the inn where they would stay for the night. When they entered the common room, Lask stopped short.

Gonamadé was sitting at a table in the corner, leaned back in his chair, feet up on the table, working his way through the box of blueberry scones in his lap.

"Where have you been?" Lask demanded.

Gonamadé looked up at him and grinned, face stained with patches of blue, and let his feet fall back to the floor.

"You did just fine without me," said the Ancient.

Myranda exchanged a glance with Lask and she slipped away with Marjusina, the two of them leaving Lask and the Gateway alone.

"Where did you go?" Lask asked him.

"I think you already know the answer to that," replied Gonamadé, his expression dark. "I am sorry to have caused you that pain."

"What was it?"

"The Gate to Hell can never be closed without a willing sacrifice; that was proven long ago. In order to close the Gate, I had to let it pull me in."

Lask's face grew dark as he realized that what he'd felt had been what the Gateway must have experienced a hundredfold. Gonamadé, however, just grinned.

"But when you're as good and important as myself," the Ancient continued, "The stay is never very long."

Lask sat down in the chair across from him and said,

"I'm glad you're alright."

Gonamadé smiled.

"I wouldn't want to lose you," Lask told him.

The Gateway's grin widened by a few teeth.

"I fear, however, that this is far from over," Lask said. "The Hydras will surely vow war."

"Of course they will." The Gateway looked across the table at him, taking in his worried expression. "Don't worry about the trials of tomorrow. You of all people should know that things have a way of working out in the end." He gave a cryptic sort of smile, then pushed the box across the table. "Scone?"

APPENDIX

The Kingdom of Etheria

See map on following page

Bodies of Water

1. The Lake of Goltor
2. The River Euphran
3. Echalan's Lake
4. The River D'hae
5. The Seeing Lake
6. Temticìl's River
7. The Bay of Belsair
8. The Lokarian Ocean
9. Castar's Pool

Forests and Plains

10. The Carthonian Forest
11. The Finistriel Forest
12. The Woods of Correneth
13. The Plain of Camulis

Mountain Ranges and Cliffs

14. The High Peaks
15. The Arayans
16. The Fallas Cliffs
17. The Therakas

Locations

18. Lask's home
19. The High King's Castle
20. Denmahi
21. Delures
22. The United's Camp
23. The Gate
24. Scoarin's Lair
25. Finistrì
26. Farisdon
27. Cranasvar
28. Allerak
29. The Griffin Roost
30. Tansfarac
31. Chai Karan's Palace
32. Sandina
33. Caladon
34. Arajei
35. The Circle of Theravian
36. The Fortress of the Hydra King
37. The Éredlé's Glade
38. The Falls of Eshalloth

The Kingdom Of
Etheria
28
30
15
31
6
5
10
7
32
8
N
13
16
35
33
34

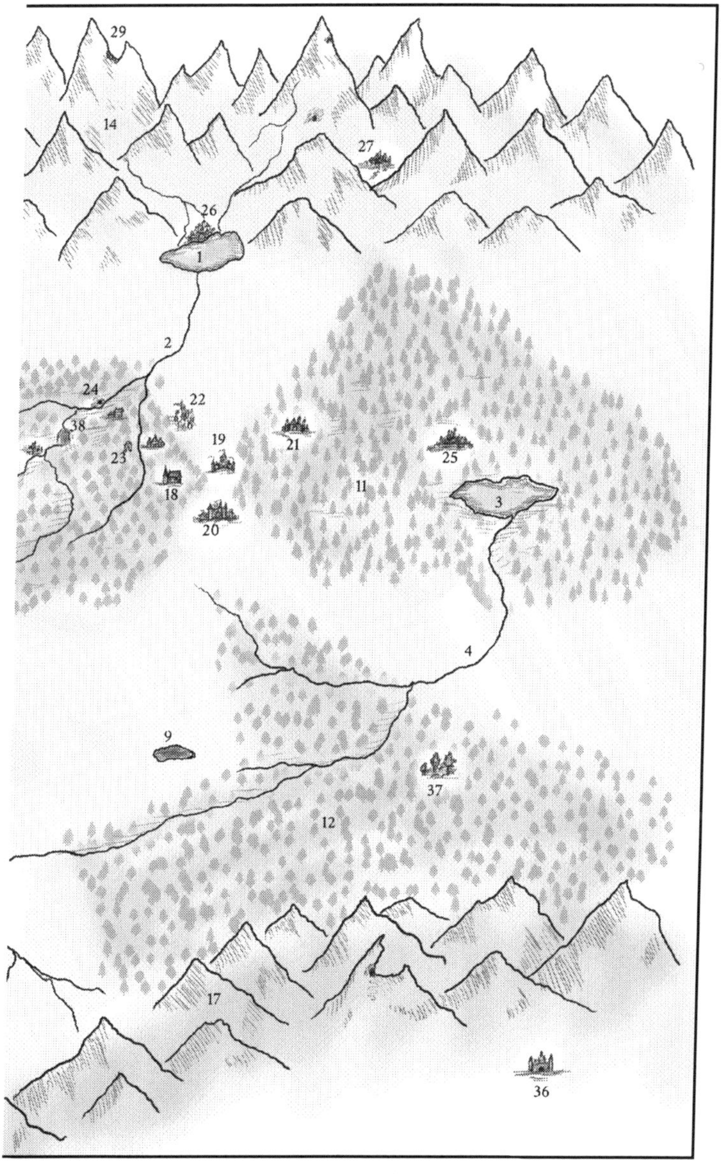
29
14
27
26
1
2
24
22
38
21
19
25
23
18
11
3
20
4
9
37
12
17
36

The Aetherian Script

For a complete dictionary and grammatical guide for the Aetherian language, visit ehkindred.com

Glossary and Pronunciation Guide

Note: The phonetic transcriptions are written according to the Etherian accent, specifically the dialect of the central kingdom.

Abadar ['æb·ə·dɑ̤ɽ] (AB-uh-dar) Aetherian name for one's grandfather.

Aborzen ['æb·ɽ̩·zɪn] (AB-er-zin) uncle of Lask and Malachi, an explorer who attempted a voyage to the West and never returned.

Adalar ['æd·ə·lɑɽ] (AD-uh-lar) one of the Hydra Kings, grandfather of Cazour.

Adar ['æ·dɑ̤ɽ] (AD-ahr) Atherian name for one's father.

Adelina [æd·ə·'li·nə] (ad-uh-LEE-nuh) sister of Falron, one of the dragons taken by the Mirror of Dùmsaro.

Adverett ['æd·vɛɽ·ɪt] (AD-ver-it) leader of the Phoenixes.

Aetherian [ai·'θɛɽ·i·ɪn] (ai-THEHR-ee-in) the Ancient Etherian language.

Airda ['eɽ·də] (AIR-duh) a centauress, daughter of Polian, member of the United council.

Ajikhan ['ɑ·ʐi·kɑn] (AH-shee-kon) a dragon in the eastern regions of Earth, who sheltered Malachi and later Scoarin.

Aldebaran ['ɐl·də·bɛɽ·ɪn] (ALL-duh-bair-in) a hydra, second in command to the Hydra King.

Androla ['æn·dɽo·lə] (AN-dro-luh) a Terwinus who aided the United.

Arajei ['eɽ·ə·ʐi] (AIR-uh-shee) the largest city in Etheria, a huge trading center with a large harbor, home of Vatron.

Arayan Mountains ['ɐɽ·e·ʎɪn] (AR-uh-yin) a chain of mountains, which surround Chai Karan's valley.

Ari ['eɽ·i] (AIR-ee) a nickname for Ariana.

Ariana [eɽ·i·'ɐn·ə] (air-ee-AHN-uh) the Dreamweaver, daughter of Salazar and Rhia.

Asmodeus [as·mo·'de·əs] (az-moh-DAY-uss) the leader of the Moranters, brother of Kairn.

Atabax ['æt·ə·bæks] (AT-uh-backs) a captain who once sailed with Aborzen, and the only member of the crew recovered after the Sea Serpent attack on their voyage to the West.

Atlanta [at·'læn·tə] (at-LAN-tuh) the queen of Letiana.

Autrial ['aʊ·tɽi·ɛl] (OW-tree-el) one of the brightest stars in the Etherian sky, part of the griffin constellation.

Belsair ['bɛl·seɽ] (BELL-sair) the bay on the western coast of Etheria.

Caledria [kə·'lɛd·ɽi·ə] (kuh-LED-ree-uh) the name of the Ancient Mystery.

Calglenn ['kɐl·glɪn] (KALL-glen) the king of Kwynn.

Calliban ['kæl·ə·bɪn] (KAL-uh-bin) a dragon, son of Scoarin, who prides himself on being the fastest flyer in the Kyn.

Camulis ['kæm·u·lɪs] (KAM-oo-liss) a large plain in southwestern Etheria, containing the majority of the kingdom's farmland, also the land of the Centaurs.

Capperith ['kæp·əɽ·ɪθ] (KAP-er-ith) the captain of the Etherian Army.

Carthonian Forest [kɐɽ·'θo·ni·ɪn] (Kar-THO-nee-in) a forest consisting mainly of Eurydicens, oaks, beeches, and other hardwoods, owned by the Somadar, home to several dragons and a number of tenants.

Castar ['kæs·tɑ̤ɽ] (KAS-tar) 1. a demon from the Void, who resided in Castar's Pool, and was banished back to the Void by Lu`corian. 2. the Pool of Castar, a small pond that is a hole in the fabric of the world. The water is so deep it touches the Void, absorbing its magic.

Cazour ['kɐ·zoɽ] (KAH-zor) the Hydra King, tyrant of the Barren Region.

Cerae ['seɽ·ai] (SAIR-ahee) a soldier in the Etherian army, married to Maresyn, favored by Lask.

Chai Karan ['tʃai 'kɐɽ·ɪn] (CHAHEE KAR-in) the name of the Ancient Time, a drokamerdor and the leader of the Drokamerdian race.

Correneth ['koɽ·ɪ·nɛθ] (KOR-in-eth) a forest consisting mainly of spruce, pines, and other conifers, territory of the Unicorns.

Delures [dɛl·'uɽ·ɛs] (dell-OOR-ehs) a large town east of the Etherian castle, city of the Eredar.

Denmahi [dɛn·'mɐ·hi] (den-MAH-hee) a city south of the Etherian castle, second largest city in Etheria, city of the Somadar.

D'hae ['dhai] (DHAHEE) the longest river in Etheria, beginning at Echalan's Lake, winding through the Woods of Correneth and the southeastern portion of the Plain of Camulis.

Diem ['di·əm] (DEE-um) the phoenix who saved Lask's life during the war with Galator.

Drake ['dɽek] (DRAIK) a soldier in the Etherian Army.

Drokamerdor [dɽɐk·ə·'meɽ·doɽ] (drok-uh-MAIR-dohr) a race of Etheria, led by Chai Karan, having the bodies of horses, the head and wings of a dragon, and the tail of a scorpion.

Dùmsaro [dum·'sɐɽ·o] (doom-SAR-oh) the title of the oldest (and therefore most powerful) Merrus in Etheria at any given time.

Echalan's Lake [ɛk·'hɐ·lɪnz] (ek-HAH-lins) the largest lake in Etheria, head of the River D'hae.

Ecthallia [ɛk·'θɐl·i·ə] (eck-THAL-ee-uh) the lieutenant of the Etherian Army.

Elinsara [ɛl·ɪn·'sɐɽ·ə] (el-in-SAR-uh) the Aetherian title and surname of the Head Ambassador.

Eredar ['ɛɽ·ə·dɐ̤ɽ] (AIR-uh-dahr) the Aetherian title and surname for the Builder.

Éredlé ['eɽ·ə·dle] (AIR-uh-dlay) the title of the Unicorn leader.

Eshalloth [ɛz·'hɐ·ləθ] (ez-HAH-luth) the largest waterfall in Etheria, found on the River Euphran. The caves behind it were home to the dragon Navar, and where Forge and Lask were raised in their youth.

Estar ['ɛs·tɐ̤ɽ] (ESS-tahr) an elected leader of an Etherian city, town, or village, much like a mayor.

Etheria [ɛθ·'ɔ·ɽi·ə] (eth-EH-ree-uh) Land of the Immortals.

Euphran [ʎu·fɽɪn] ['ɛ·u·fɽɐn] (YOO-frin) (in earlier Ages: EH-oo-fron) a river in Etheria, beginning at the Lake of Goltor, passing through the Carthonian, and emptying into the Bay of Belsair.

Eurydicen [ʎəɽ·'ɪd·sɛn] (yur-ID-iss-in) the sacred tree species of Etheria.

Faileas ['fel·i·əs] (FAIL-ee-uhs) the Archiver (Sìrodar) during the reign of Lavancer.

Fallas Cliffs ['fɐl·əs] (FALL-uhs) the black cliffs on the Lokarian Ocean haunted by the Wraiths.

Falron ['fɐl·ɽɑn] (FAL-ron) a black dragon, mate of Scoarin.

Falsanthur [fal·'san·θɽ̩] (fal-SAN-ther) father of Navar, a dragon taken by the Mirror of Dùmsaro and then magically changed to human form on Earth.

Famas['fa·məs] (FAH-mus) the second host of the Gateway, a human.

Farisdon ['fɛɽ·ɪs·dɒn] (FAIR-iss-don) a large fishing city in the High Peaks on the Lake of Goltor, third largest city in Etheria, city of the Sìrodar.

Ferratine ['fɛɽ·ə·tin] (FAIR-uh-teen) an uncommon metal, the strongest known metal found within Etheria, very light when forged properly, extremely desirable for armor.

Fildahorr ['fɪl·dɐ·hoɽ] (FIL-dah-hor) Guardian of the Tress, leader of the Warauls.

Finistriel Forest [fɪn·'ɪs·tɽi·ɛl] (fen-ISS-tree-uhl) a forest consisting of both hardwoods and softwoods, home of the Fairies.

Finistrì ['fɪn·ɪs·tɽi] (FEN-iss-tree) the city of the Fairies.

Forge ['foɽʒ] (FORGE) the nickname for Josten, general of the Etherian Army, best friend of Lask.

Galator ['gal·ə·toɽ] (GAL-uh-tor) a griffin, the younger brother of Ossifer, rebelled against Etheria, fled to Earth in an attempt to raise a mortal army, slain by Lask.

Gelfin ['gɛl·fɪn] (GEL-fin) a soldier of Vortearigan, held captive by the United.

Giselle [ʒɪ·'sɛl] (jih-SELL) a fairy, secretary to Julius in Finistrì.

Goltor ['gol·toɽ] (GOHL-tor) the second largest lake in Etheria, found in the High Peaks, beginning of the River Euphran.

Gonamadé [gɑn·ə·'ma·de] (gon-uh-MAH-deh) the name of the Ancient Gateway.

Hèadara [he·ə·'dɐɽ·ə] (hey-uh-DAHR-uh) the title of the Dragon leader.

Hèit ['he·ɪt] (HEY-it) the title of the Centaur leader.

Hydrellia [hɪ·'dɽe·li·ə] (hid-RAY-lee-uh) a town on the Euphran River destroyed by Vortearigan, birthplace of Lask.

Josten ['ʒɑs·tɪn] (JOSS-tin) the real (and rarely used) name of Forge.

Julius ['ʒu·li·əs] (JOO-lee-uhs) the Fairy General.

Kaeron ['kai·ɽɑn] (KAHI-ron) a young griffin who found the Spring of Life and drowned in its waters, the mythical origin of the griffin constellation in the Etherian sky.

Kairn ['keɽn] (KAIRN) the brother of Asmodeus.

Keppàs [kɛ·'pɐs] (keh-PAHS) a common Etherian vegetable.

Kunia ['ku·ni·ə] (KOO-nee-uh) an Etherian coin, made of copper.

Kwynn ['kwɪn] (KWIN) the mortal kingdom north of Letiana.

Kyn ['kɪn] (KIN) the Dragon Kyn of Etheria, or more generally, a group of dragons.

Lask Maveran Somadar ['læsk mə·'vɛɽ·ɪn 'so·mə·dɐ̤ɽ] (LASK muh-VAIR-in SO-muh-dahr) the fourth Somadar of Etheria, son of Luke and Sasha, younger brother of Malachi, husband of Myranda, father of Salazar, Uniter of the races and head of the United council.

Lavancer [lə·'væn·sɽ̩] (luh-VAN-sir) the High King of Etheria, fourth monarch of Etheria.

Letiana [lɛ·ti·'ɐn·ə] (leh-tee-AHN-uh) the mortal kingdom south of Kwynn, home of Salazar and his family.

Lirax ['liɽ·æks] (LEER-ax) the owner of the Silver Shanty tavern in Arajei.

Lokarian Ocean [lo·'kɐɽ·i·ɪn] (loh-KAR-ee-in) the ocean separating Eastern and Western Etheria, home of the Sea Serpents and Merfolk.

Lothanvar ['lɑ·θɪn·vɐɽ] (LAW-thin-vahr) a powerful Merrus who created the Mirror of Dùmsaro.

Lu'corian [lu·'koɽ·i·ɪn] (loo-COR-ee-in) The First Somadar, husband of Mara, father of Siratrian.

Luke ['luk] (LOOK) the third Somadar of Etheria, unfaithful husband of Sasha, abusive father of Malachi and Lask, brought the kingdom to the point of civil war, killed by Vortearigan.

Malachi ['mæl·ə·kai] (MAL-uh-kahee) son of Luke, elder brother of Lask, made several attempts to kill his brother, culminating in the accidental murder of King Sendanten, which led to his banishment on Earth until he later returned to aid the United.

Maléchian [mə·'le·tʃi·ɪn] (muh-LAY-chee-in) the personal name of the Mirror of Dùmsaro.

Maresyn ['mɛɽ·ə·sɪn] (MAIR-uh-sin) the chief scouting officer in the Etherian Army, husband of Cerae, favored by Lask.

Mata ['ma·tə] (MAH-tuh) Atherian name for one's mother.

Merrus, pl. **Merrui** ['mɛɽ·əs] ['mɛɽ·u·i] (MAIR-us) (MAIR-oo-ee) a Spirit bound for Hell, but trapped in Etheria, capable of amassing dark magic in correlation to the severity of their crimes in life and the duration of time they remain in Etheria.

Messalo [mɛ·'sa·lo] (meh-SAH-lo) a griffin, friend to Marjusina, accompanied Lask and his companions to the Spring of Life.

Mìtov ['mi·tav] (MEE-tahv) a hydra.

Montevale ['mɑn·tə·vel] (MON-tuh-vail) a fairy sea captain, cousin of Sutonius.

Moranter ['moɽ·ɐn·tɛɽ] (MOR-ahn-tair) a race of Etheria, large lizards with manes and, if male, beards.

Morpheus ['moɽ·fi·əs] (MOR-fee-us) a griffin, the son of Ossifer, a member of the United council.

Myranda [mə·'ɽæn·də] (muh-RAN-duh) wife of Lask, mother of Salazar, a mortal of Kwynn who was given Immortality by Lask.

Navar [nə·'vɑɽ] (nuh-VAR) an orphaned dragon, raised by Siratrian, later the adoptive father of Lask and Forge.

Ossifer ['ɑs·ɪ·fɽ̩] (AHS-uh-fer) the leader of the Griffins, father of Morpheus.

Polian ['po·li·ɪn] (POHL-ee-in) the leader of the Centaurs, a member of the United council.

Ranseor [ɽan·'se·oɽ] (ran-SAY-or) father of Vatron, one

of the dragons taken by the Mirror of Dùmsaro.

Réasdar ['ɽe·əs·dɐ̤ɽ] (RAY-uss-dahr) Aetherian title for the High King, occasionally serving as a surname of the king.

Rekan [ɽɛ·'kɐn] (reh-KAHN) the title of the griffin leader.

Rhia ['ɽi·ə] (REE-uh) the adopted daughter of Asmodeus, wife of Salazar, mother of Ariana, a mortal of Kwynn who was given Immortality by Salazar.

Rosecca [ɽos·'ɛk·ə] (rohs-EK-uh) the daughter of Muras, leader of the Unicorns.

Salazar ['sæl·ə·zɐɽ] (SAL-uh-zahr) son of Lask, husband of Rhia, father of Ariana, resided with the Warauls during his teen years, ambassador to Letiana after Lask's return to Etheria.

Salìt [sɐ·'lit] (sah-LEET) the chief medical officer and surgeon in the Etherian Army.

Sandina [san·'di·nə] (san-DEE-nuh) a village on the Plain of Camulis.

Sasha ['sɐ·ʃə] (SAH-shuh) the wife of Luke, mother of Malachi and Lask.

Sayden ['se·dɪn] (SAY-din) the former home of the

Warauls in Etheria.

Scelesto [skə·'lɛs·to] (skuh-LESS-toh) the leader of the Wraiths.

Scoarin [sko·'ɐɽ·ɪn] (skoh-AHR-in) the leader of the Dragon Kyn, mate to Falron, mother of Calliban.

Selat ['sɛ·lat] (SEL-at) a hydra.

Sendanten [sɪn·'dæn·tɪn] (sin-DAN-tin) the third High King of Etheria, father of Lavancer, poisoned and slain by Malachi.

Seppish ['sɛ·pɪʃ] (SEH-pish) a waraul, friend of Salazar and Fildahorr.

Sergar ['seɽ·gaɽ] (SAIR-gar) a hydra brutally executed by Aldebaran at the command of Cazour.

Serin ['seɽ·ɪn] (SAIR-in) the term for each of the seven divisions of the Etherian Army. Each Serin has a primary function; cavalry, scouts, archers, etc.

Siratrian [sɽ·'æt·ɽi·ɪn] (sir-AT-ree-in) the second Somadar, son of Lu`corian and Mara, father of Luke and Aborzen, foster father of the dragon Navar, renowned herbalist.

Sirezo [sɪɽ·'e·zo] (sir-EH-zo) the mortal who crossed into

Etheria in pursuit of the Dragons summoned Lothanvar to create the Mirror of Dùmsaro.

Sìrodar ['siɽ·o·da̤ɽ] (SEER-oh-dar) the Aetherian title and surname of the Archiver.

Socadan [sɑk·ə·dɪn] (SOK-uh-din) a wizard.

Somadar ['so·mə·dɐ̤ɽ] (SOHM-uh-dahr) Aetherian title of the Protector, occasionally used as a surname of the individual holding the office.

Somadàrsath [so·mə·'dɐɽ·sɛθ] (sohm-uh-DAHR-seth) a modification of the word Somadar with the addition of the Aetherian suffix –sath, meaning "blood" or "bloodline." Used to indicate a descendent of Lu`corian who has not held or is not holding the office of the Somadar.

Sutonius [su·'ton·i·əs] (soo-TOHN-ee-us) a fairy, second in command to the Fairy General, Julius.

Tarquinius [taɽ·'kwɪn·i·əs] (tar-KWIN-ee-us) the third host of the Gateway, a fairy.

Terwinus, pl. **Terwini** [teɽ·wɪn·əs] [teɽ·wɪn·i] (TAIR-win-us) (TER-win-ee) a good Spirit bound for Heaven, trapped in Etheria by unfinished business.

Theramancer ['θeɽ·ə·man·sɽ] (THAIR-uh-man-sir) Lask's stallion and warhorse.

Theravian [θəɽ·'ɔ·vi·ən] (thur-EH-vee-in) the son of Arister, Leader of the Centaurs, died in battle, honored with the stone Circle of Theravian, which serves as the meeting place of the Centaurs.

Vatron ['væt·ɽən] (VAT-ruhn) a dragon from Arajei, friend and advisor of Scoarin.

Verdin ['vɪɽ·dɪn] (VER-din) an Etherian scout and messenger.

Vortearigan [voɽ·'teɽ·ɪ·gɪn] (vor-TAIR-igg-in) an Etherian rebel who slew Luke and crippled the kingdom, then went into hiding to later lead a war against the United.

Waraul [wə·'ɽaʊl] (wuh-ROWL) a wolf-like race of Etheria, dwelling on Earth to guard the Gate.

18969025R00182

Made in the USA
Charleston, SC
30 April 2013